"Sorry, I —working out." As she finished speaking, her eyes skittered away from the towel fastened precariously low on Daniel's hips. She saw his biceps bulge slightly as he gripped the doorjam.

His gaze slowly traveling the length of her sheer cotton nightgown, he said, "I swear, Kerith, you are the most beautiful woman I've ever seen." His voice was soft, anguished. "Having you here and not being able to touch you is the sweetest torture I've ever known."

Sweet torture. Yes, that it was, Kerith thought, her body pulsing with sensual excitement. "Daniel, I—"

"No, you don't have to repeat all the reasons you can't," he said. "I made a promise, and I'll keep it. But if you ever change your mind, I'll make sure you don't regret it." He stepped back into his bedroom, preparing to shut the door, but Kerith's whisper stopped him cold.

"Is that a promise?"

Dawn Carroll's first love is singing; in fact, she performed semiprofessionally for many years. One of her most memorable moments was her unscheduled solo while performing in an opera with Beverly Sills—Dawn came in too soon! Beverly apparently thought it was hilarious; Dawn nearly died.

After her second child was born, Dawn decided a career change was in order. Writing, she found, gave her an outlet for her creative urges and allowed her to spend more time at home. Now all the passion and pathos of her singing is channeled into her characters, as *Code Name: Casanova*—her first Harlequin Temptation—demonstrates.

Code Name Casanova

DAWN CARROLL

Harlequin Books

TORONTO • NEW YORK • LONDON
AMSTERDAM • PARIS • SYDNEY • HAMBURG
STOCKHOLM • ATHENS • TOKYO • MILAN

For April and Joey,
who have gracefully borne the trials
of having a mother who must write.
And for James,
my friend, my partner . . . my love.

Published September 1989

ISBN 0-373-25368-0

1

"HELLO, CASANOVA." The woman's voice was low, cultured, vaguely seductive. "This is Lucretia. I need you."

Even after six months the mere sound of that voice sent a spurt of adrenaline into Daniel Avanti's bloodstream. Irritation flared as he tightened his grip on the telephone receiver and quelled a strong impulse to simply hang up. *Easy Avanti, you're a civilian now. She doesn't control your life.*

"Sorry, no Casanova at this number," he drawled in a calculatedly sensual bass. He'd always hated the code name; even if he couldn't deny earning it. Too many memories best forgotten echoed hollowly in the sound of that name. He wondered if God provided special expiation for the sins a man committed in the name of protecting his country.

Tilting back in his oversized executive chair, he stared broodingly at the crystalline Las Vegas morning just outside the glass wall of his private office. Specters of the past counseled him to end the call, but curiosity teased him into asking, "What is it this time, Lucretia? Seducing secrets out of some lonely lady scientist? A foreign diplomat's wife?"

An abrupt snort of reproof sounded clearly, belying the thousands of miles that separated him from the anonymous office in Washington, D.C., which housed a main artery of the nation's secret intelligence network. "Sarcasm doesn't suit you, my boy. You're much more useful when you're charming. Actually, there is a lady involved and she requires special handling. The request came from out of town."

Which means another agency, Daniel translated silently. *Probably not even one of ours.*

"They want someone to get close to her, intimate surveillance. Top priority." Lucretia sounded less seductive and more like her old autocratic self.

The corner of Daniel's mouth quirked derisively. Intimate surveillance, ha! Seasoned agents more accurately termed it pillow talk. It was one of the main reasons he had turned his back on a career spanning fifteen years. It was also the primary reason he'd remained celibate since coming home.

Not that temptation didn't call occasionally, he qualified, as he looked through the window. A leggy brunette in breathtaking tight jogging shorts and tank top waited while one of his mechanics drove a slope-nosed red Maserati out onto the front drive of Avanti's Foreign Auto Service. When his man alighted to courteously hold the door for her, she did a bend from the waist to stow her purse behind the seat and the way those shorts rode up in the back made Daniel's breath catch. Heaven only knew how his mechanic kept it all together.

And yet, even as the first stirrings of desire sent warm tentacles through his midsection, he couldn't help remembering the faint queasiness that came the morning after a night of emotionless sex.

"Are you thinking about it?" Lucretia prompted, reminding him of the active part she had played in making the code name Casanova a legend in the world of counterintelligence—and in making Daniel Avanti a man who could barely face himself in the mirror when he'd left active field duty two years ago. Not even the flatteringly powerful position the agency had given him in administration had been able to blot out the memory of what he had been.

"You're forgetting one little detail," he replied coldly. "I no longer work for you. The family business is operating quite solidly in the black, and I have no intention of leaving it. Why me, anyway? You must have dozens of loyal young studs who can handle this kind of job."

"We've tried some of the others, the lady wasn't buying. She's somewhat aloof, when it comes to men."

"What's the matter? Your pretty boys losing their touch?"

Ignoring his jibe, Lucretia continued. "The job was made for you, my friend. Not only are you the most charming devil that ever walked this earth, you also have the advantage of proximity. The subject happens to be one of your customers. Her name is Kerith Anders and she owns Classique Limousine Service. Sound familiar?"

Daniel scowled as the full implication of Lucretia's unexpected call dawned on him. "Lord, when I think of the megabytes of data stored in that computer of yours, it scares the hell out of me. Next you'll tell me we share the same blood type."

Lucretia gave her rusty imitation of a chuckle. "No, but we show every indication that you'll be compatible. *Do* you know her?"

Daniel searched his memory briefly. "I know of her, but I've never met her. Classique is one of my largest accounts, but most of our business is conducted by bookkeepers and secretaries. I heard she inherited the business from old Gus Anders when he died. My secretary said there was quite a scandal when they got married. Seems Gus was nearly old enough to be her grandfather."

"You see?" Lucretia sounded triumphant. "You already know something about her. Getting closer should require very little effort. And you wouldn't have to neglect your beloved business in the least. The perfect setup, right?"

"Wrong!" Daniel surged to his feet, then remembered his considerable height wouldn't give him an advantage over the phone. His handsome features hardened in a frown as he sat down again and tried to control his temper. It was a weakness Lucretia had taken advantage of too often in the past. That and the guilt. "Look, I'm not going to waste time arguing with you. The answer is no, and it always will be. Goodbye, Lucretia, dear." He started to hang up, when her voice rang out, naming an amount of money that made him jerk the receiver back to his ear.

"I thought you said the job was surveillance. That kind of money usually means heavy trouble."

Lucretia laughed, the dry, humorless exclamation of a hyena. "Retirement is making you overly suspicious, my friend. Did you consider that the lady might simply have some very wealthy friends in high places?"

"Someone you owe a favor, no doubt."

"Not really. Think of it more as a hands-across-the-sea gesture. Liaison for a foreign cousin. I can't tell you more than that, for now, but I do have some fascinating background on the lady in question. I can have the dossier on your desk in thirty minutes."

The short delivery time didn't impress Daniel. To someone with Lucretia's power, being distanced by a continent was a minor inconvenience.

On the other hand, a local businesswoman under the scrutiny of foreign powers could definitely be intriguing. Daniel actually caught himself teetering on the edge of acceptance before he recognized the trap Lucretia had laid. "Keep your damned dossier. I told you, I'm not working for you anymore." It gave him a great deal of satisfaction to hang up before she could protest.

But when he returned from a business lunch later that afternoon and found a large manila envelope locked inside his briefcase, he wasn't really surprised. Lucretia's arrogance was equaled only by her persistence. Nor could he prevent himself from opening the envelope. If anything, his curiosity had grown stronger in the intervening hours, as his mind had had time to play with the possibilities of the situation. The woman involved was a business associate, after all. Didn't he owe it to himself to find out what was going on?

His interest was piqued even further when he saw the first eight-by-ten color photo included with the thin sheaf of papers. The woman captured there had the most arresting face he had encountered in a long time. Not beautiful in the American sense of wholesome perfection, she possessed instead exotic sensuality and a captivating air of mystery. Her hair was a silky, chin-length cap the color of fine Belgian toffee. The slightly up-tilted eyes were almost almond-shaped, their deep golden hue reminiscent of wild honey. Elegantly high cheekbones stretched her gold-tinted skin taut and a delicately patrician nose gave her a vaguely haughty look.

There was nothing haughty about her mouth, however. The full, peach-tinted lips had a pouting sensuality that tempted a man with wildly disparate promises of innocent pleasure and wanton ecstasy.

So Lucretia's gigolos had struck out, Daniel mused with a contemptuous smile. Not hard to understand, now that he'd seen the target's picture. He could easily imagine her being well-versed in the art of rebuffing men's advances; she'd probably been practicing most of her life!

There had been a time when special agent Casanova would have considered her an irresistible challenge, but Daniel wasn't hooked until he flipped to the second glossy photo in the stack. This portrait was a tribute to the thoroughness and competence of Lucretia's photographer. That he had caught his subject in an unguarded moment was immediately evident.

Although the second picture was a close-up head shot, like the first, a shocking vulnerability had replaced the continental sophistication of the previous photo. Something intensely private was exposed on that chemically treated piece of paper: a raw flash of emotion totally at odds with the cosmopolitan poise of the woman in the other photo. Seeing it affected him like a blow to the heart. He'd seen that look before on another lovely face. Angelina's face. The passage of time had dimmed exact recall of her features, but nothing could erase the memory of that look.

Damn Lucretia. She couldn't have found out about Angelina. Only his immediate family and a few old friends such as Alita Spencer had witnessed that painful episode. But then, Lucretia was well known for her instinctive knowledge of a man's weaknesses. Had she anticipated his reaction? Was she capitalizing on the fact that the great Casanova, purportedly heartless when it came to women, had ultimately been destroyed by a backlash of guilt?

Daniel impatiently drummed his fingers on the desktop as he considered his options. He could just relock the briefcase and forget the whole thing. That would be the rational thing to do, if he wanted to keep Lucretia and her memories in the past where they belonged.

He gazed around, taking in the wood and leather elegance of his private office. The office he'd inherited from his father, along with an auto-repair service that cosseted some of the most valuable automobiles in the state, maybe in the whole country. The paneled walls were lined with photographs of the rich and famous who entrusted Avanti's with the care of their exotic machines. This was important to him now, along with the careful mending of the precious family ties he'd so ruthlessly severed seventeen years ago. He'd be a fool to let Lucretia into even one tiny corner of his life. And yet . . .

He looked again at the exotically beautiful face frozen in a moment of utter defenselessness. What was her name again? He shuffled the papers until he found the basic stats sheet and read, Subject Name: Kerith (pronounced Care-ith) Marie Anders. Maiden name: Braun. Below that was a personal note from the investigator, stating the origin of the first name was unknown and that Braun was the surname given to her by the nuns at the orphanage where she'd been raised.

An orphan. That piece of news gave Daniel pause. He'd never known an orphan before, and he was ill equipped to guess at how it would feel to be one. Even during all those years of deliberate separation from his family, he'd always had the certainty of his roots, his heritage to fall back on in the lonely times.

If Lucretia's information was correct, Kerith Anders had no one. Except, of course, for the rich and powerful friends who wanted her watched, Daniel amended with a grim smile. Could they be the cause of the sharp melancholy in that second photo? Even if they weren't, it was still possible that their interference wouldn't be in the lady's best interests. He knew a sudden, forceful urge to protect Kerith Anders from Lucretia and her sort. And the only way he could do that would be by accepting the assignment and finding out what the hell was going on.

He held up the two pictures, side by side, and studied them, feeling again a sympathetic ache in the region of his heart. "Well, Kerith Marie Anders," he murmured softly. "I think you've just acquired a champion. I hope I don't live to regret it."

With that decision made, he sat forward and reached for the telephone. His first order of business would be getting close to this woman who obviously wasn't in the market for male company. And he knew just the person to arrange it. Ali Spencer was a chauffeur at Classique. And when it came to matchmaking, she was almost as compulsive as his mother. All he'd have to do was drop a hint or two to Ali about his utter fascination with her boss . . .

KERITH PROPELLED HERSELF out of the pool's refreshingly cool water, her hands braced on the tiled coping. With fluid grace, she came to a standing position on the brick patio and raised her arms to the shimmering blue expanse of the morning sky. Water sluiced down her golden nakedness like sunlight sliding over silk, highlighting the becoming curves and hollows of her supple body. Head back, eyes closed, spine arched, she offered herself like a pagan to the warmth of the late-August sun. She remained like that, reveling in the freedom of the moment, her soul soaring like a captive bird unexpectedly set free.

And then the intrusive chime of the front doorbell brought her tumbling back to earth. Instinctively, her arms swooped down to shield her nakedness, but she caught herself at the last instant and straightened resolutely. *No one can see you*, she chided herself silently, her eyes sweeping the high brick walls surrounding her backyard.

Still, she retrieved a thick, white terry-cloth robe from a nearby chaise lounge and shrugged into it as she headed through the house to the front door, her bare feet leaving damp impressions on plush ivory carpeting. As she squinted to look out the peephole, she heard a car door slam and the roar of an engine accelerating away, but the porch and the street in front of her house appeared to be uninhabited.

Had she imagined the bell? But no, there had been the slamming door and the sound of that retreating engine. She opened the door a crack and checked the neighborhood. It looked deserted, which was normal. This quiet suburb was primarily inhabited by the night people of Las Vegas. People here were performers and dealers who began their workday as the moon rose and slept when the hot dessert sun burned over the city.

Satisfied she was unobserved, Kerith stepped out and nearly tripped over the potted plant someone had left on her welcome mat. With a muttered exclamation she bent to pick it up . . . then froze as her brain registered and identified the star-shaped flowers nestled among long, slender leaves. A casual observer might have dismissed them as common wildflowers. Not Kerith. She knew that this particular flower grew wild only in the Alps, but more importantly, to her they were an unwelcome reminder of a time in her life she had worked hard to forget.

"Edelweiss," she whispered in a stricken voice. Like a sleepwalker she rose and carried the plant inside, placing it on the coffee table before sinking onto the couch, unmindful of the damage her damp robe might do to the satin-brocade upholstery. "Edelweiss," she murmured again, reaching with one shaking finger to stroke the fuzzy, white petals that surrounded a bright yellow center. The flower bobbed gently on its stem and the colors blurred before her eyes as memories surged up with poignant clarity.

Her fifth birthday. That's when it had begun; when this small, unassuming flower had begun to carry a deeper significance in her life. She still remembered the day with painful clarity: the summons to Mother Superior's office; the long walk down a cold hallway on trembling legs; the grave expression on Mother's softly aged face . . .

"Come in child and sit down."

Relaxing a little at the lack of steel in the old nun's tone, Kerith had climbed onto the hard wooden chair positioned in front of Mother's ancient oaken desk.

"I have something to show you," the nun went on once Kerith was settled, her thin legs sticking straight out over the edge of the chair. "God has seen fit to bless you with a benefactor and I think you are old enough to know about it."

Of course, being five, Kerith had assumed the envelope handed to her had come from God Himself, in spite of Mother's vague explanations about anonymous gifts. It wasn't until much later that she began to wonder about the donor of the cashier's check inside the envelope. And wondering had led to wild hopes and fantasies that had inevitably given way to disillusionment and frustration, because her benefactor had remained a maddening enigma, despite her most determined sleuthing. Not even her occasional midnight forays into the orphanage's locked files had ever produced any information.

The check itself had been drawn from a numbered Swiss-bank account each year on her birthday. No names, no signatures, except the official scrawl of the bank president. The only clue she'd ever had was the blank piece of paper folded around the check, an expensive piece of vellum embossed with an edelweiss.

Kerith shivered and pulled her robe more securely around her. Edelweiss. For a time, she'd actually dared to hope that someone would come to claim her one day, just like Daddy Warbucks in *Little Orphan Annie*. But the years passed and no one came. Edelweiss had never offered more than monetary benefaction and the autocratic arrangement of her life. She shivered again as a phantom of the old pain touched her soul, followed quickly by the inevitable flash of resentment. Hadn't Edelweiss had enough of manipulating her life back then? Why this unexpected reminder after years of silence?

Twelve years, to be exact. Twelve years since the last check had arrived on her eighteenth birthday, along with a scholarship to a frighteningly foreign-sounding American university. It had been the final step in the long series of directives that had ruled her childhood and shaped her into the woman she was today. She'd taken the irresistible offer of a prepaid formal education at the cost of accepting, once again, the life-changing decisions of a person she had never even seen. What if she had turned the scholarship down . . . ?

The ivory phone resting on the end table near her elbow rang twice before the sound penetrated her troubled thoughts. Still slightly distracted, she reached for it and answered in the language of her childhood. "*Do isch Kerith.*"

"Hello? Kerith, is that you?" Ali Spencer's familiar contralto quickly brought the present back into focus.

Realizing her slip, Kerith laughed self-consciously. "Sorry, Ali. I was thinking about Switzerland and automatically answered in German. What can I do for you?"

"I have a big favor to ask." Ali rarely wasted time on long preliminaries. "I promised to chauffeur a friend of mine and some of his relatives tonight, and this afternoon I fell and sprained my ankle."

Kerith groaned sympathetically. "How bad is it?"

"The doctor said to stay off it for a couple of days. That includes driving, since it's my right foot. Anyway, I checked with Charlotte and all of our drivers are busy tonight."

"Except me, the boss," Kerith put in wryly.

"Right." Ali's husky chuckle trailed off uncertainly. "I know it's asking a lot at the last minute, but this is really important. In fact, you might even think of it as good business relations. The friend I mentioned is Daniel Avanti, as in Avanti's Foreign Auto Service. His sister Annette is getting married tomorrow, and tonight Daniel and a few of his relatives are taking the groom out on the town. Sort of a bachelor party on wheels."

Kerith started to protest, but Ali quickly cut her off. "I know, it's not your run-of-the-mill contract, but you're always telling me how much you enjoyed chauffeuring before you took over administration, especially the unusual jobs. Think of this as an opportunity to brighten up one of your normally dull and lonely Friday nights."

"You'd better watch the subtle slurs on my social life, if you don't want your friends to walk," Kerith warned, reaching for the notepad and pencil she kept near the phone. "Now, where and when do I pick up these gentlemen?" Listening intently, she quickly noted Ali's instructions. "Okay, I've got it. Anything else?"

"Yeah, I agreed to drive the newlyweds from the church to the reception, and then on to the hotel where they're spending their honeymoon. I wasn't going to charge them the full rate, since I was invited to the wedding anyway, but you can take the difference out of my paycheck. They want to use the Rolls, which, if you'll recall, you agreed to when I asked two weeks ago."

"I also told you I haven't been using the Rolls much because I can't rely on it—thanks to your pal Daniel's service manager. He keeps sending it back saying it's fixed, and a few weeks later it breaks down again. If that happens during a contracted ride, my business reputation is on the line."

"I explained all that to Daniel. He said he'd look into it personally after the wedding. In the meantime, he's willing to risk the odds of the car not breaking down. You see—" Ali's voice faltered with sudden emotion. "Joe Avanti died six months ago, and Daniel's doing everything in his power to make up for the fact that Annette won't have her father to give her away at the wedding. When she mentioned her dream of riding in a Rolls-Royce, Daniel and I committed ourselves to making that dream come true."

Kerith smiled and brushed back the damp tangle of her bangs. "You and Daniel, hmm? Sounds like you're sold on this guy. Are you perhaps thinking of giving up your role as the swinging divorcée?"

Ali's startled laughter provided an answer before she spoke. "Daniel isn't that kind of friend. Although, lord knows, he's got everything a woman could want. It's just that we've known each other since we were kids— our dads were even in business together for a while— and I've never been able to think of him as anything more than a big brother." There was a significant pause. "He's definitely available, Kerith. He's also devastatingly handsome, financially secure and remarkably lacking in conceit."

Kerith was instantly on guard. "Take it easy on the glowing praise. I'm not interested."

"You never are, darn it, and you should be." Ali's voice was gently accusing now. "Gus would have been mortified at the prospect of you mourning him like this. There hasn't been one man in your life since he died, and it isn't for lack of trying on the male side of the population."

There hadn't been any men in her life before Gus, either, Kerith thought, pushing her damp bangs back from her forehead with an irritated motion. Except that near-disaster in college. But no one, not even Ali, knew that. Since Gus's death two years ago, people had attributed her lack of social life to lingering grief. Not that she didn't grieve. Gus had given her a brief taste of the dangerous sweetness of letting someone get close, of caring deeply. And then he had abandoned her in death, as surely as she had been abandoned at birth. She'd vowed not to repeat the experience.

Her eyes focused on the flowering plant sitting so innocently on her coffee table. *You see, Edelweiss? I've learned a lot since I escaped your influence.*

"You're not talking," Ali said with a nervous little laugh. "Are you mad at me for nagging? You know I only do it because I care. You're a dear friend, Kerith, in addition to being the nicest boss I've ever had."

Not going to let anyone get close, huh? a silent voice accused. Restlessly Kerith picked up the pencil, and began doodling a border of star-shaped flowers around the hastily scribbled instructions on her phone pad. Friendship with Ali was different than involvement with a man, she told herself. And even though Ali had been pushing the boundaries of that friendship lately, Kerith couldn't bring herself to halt it just yet. She'd allowed herself so few real friends in her lifetime.

"I'm not mad," she said at last. "But I wish you'd give up. My life is too busy for the kind of complications men seem to generate. And I've yet to find one worth the trouble."

"Daniel is," Ali responded promptly. "You'll see once you've met him."

"Don't count on it. I'm going to be his chauffeur tonight, and chauffeurs are generally ignored by their clients."

"Not when the chauffeur looks like you," Ali said with a knowing chuckle.

"Ali . . ." The single word was heavy with warning.

"All right, I'll quit. Especially since you're being nice enough to fill in for me. I don't know how I'm going to repay you."

"I'm willing to call it even if you'll just stop trying to sell me on the amazing Mr. Avanti."

Ali laughed again. "Don't worry, my promotion won't be needed once you meet him. He'll do all the selling himself."

WHEN DANIEL AVANTI opened the door to his trendy, two-story condominium that evening, it occurred to Kerith that Ali might have been right. The tall, raven-haired man before her looked like he'd probably be able to sell striped shorts to zebras. Not only was he blessed with the dark-eyed sensuality so typical of Latin men, but Daniel Avanti seemed to radiate the kind of innate charm that could reach out and beguile before his victim had time to react.

His eyes, the rich color of bittersweet chocolate, were meltingly intimate, his disturbingly masculine smile promised the world, and his strong, slightly aquiline nose suggested he was a man who delivered on his promises. The faint lines of experience etched on his lean, tanned face told her he was probably well into his thirties, but they only added to his compelling attractiveness. For the first time in her life, Kerith found she was unable to look away with cool disinterest.

"You must be Kerith," he murmured through that captivating smile. "I've been looking forward to meeting you."

As his deep voice caressed her ears, a soft evening breeze, still warm from the setting sun, wafted between them carrying the delicate perfume of night-blooming jasmine. Its intoxicating sweetness caused a sharp increase in her disorientation, and Kerith forced her eyes away from his face in an effort to break the spell. She quickly discovered looking at the rest of him didn't improve matters at all. He was unusually tall, probably four or five inches over six feet, and his body had the kind of lithe, toned muscularity that bespoke disciplined maintenance. Even in a simple, white sport shirt and navy slacks, he radiated urbane power and masculine confidence.

The silence between them had stretched uncomfortably, too long to repair. Kerith decided to ignore the warmth of his greeting and get back to basics. "I hope you'll enjoy your ride with Classique Limousine, Mr. Avanti," she said in her most formal chauffeur's voice. "I'll be waiting at the car whenever you're ready to leave."

Daniel watched in surprise as Kerith pivoted neatly on one heel and returned to the sparkling white Cadillac limousine parked at the curb. After the dazed once-over she'd given him at first sight, he'd expected either the subtle come-on of a woman well versed in sexual games or the flushing confusion of one of her less experienced sisters caught gazing too long at a man's attributes. Those were the reactions his appearance normally garnered. Instead he'd gotten cool dismissal, and it challenged him in a way nothing had in a long time. As he locked the door to his condo and started after Kerith, his pulse quickened in anticipation.

He walked slowly, taking time for his own detailed perusal of the woman waiting at the open rear door of the limo. Dynamite. Even better than her picture, he thought, enjoying the way the tailored gray trousers of her uniform hugged her trim waistline, and the saucy curve of her bottom. He had known she would be slightly above average height—five foot eight, according to Lucretia's report—and that she weighed around a hundred and twenty-five pounds. But not even Lucretia could have described how delightfully those pounds were distributed.

The view from the back was almost as enjoyable as the one from the front. The white shirt of her uniform was short-sleeved, an obvious concession to the extreme Las Vegas heat, but other than that it closely resembled the formal shirt worn with a tuxedo, including pin-tucked pleats and a neat, black-satin bow tie. Over it she wore a short gray vest, with a deeply scooped neckline that buttoned snugly under the rounded softness of her breasts. On her shining golden brown hair was perched a smart, gray chauffeur's cap. The entire outfit had been designed to promote an image of formal efficiency, but seeing it on Kerith's lush, womanly body made his senses stir with decidedly informal thoughts . . . like bedrooms and rumpled sheets and the musky scent of lovemaking.

A surprising thought filtered through Daniel's stirring senses. Where was that little shaft of self-disgust that normally checked his desire at this point, forcing him to continue in a more calculated route to physical satisfaction? Was it possible...? No, he wouldn't jump to any conclusions just yet; he'd see where the evening led, first.

Kerith heard Daniel's approaching footsteps and purposely kept her eyes focused on the flowering ash trees lining his street. She was still reeling a bit from the aftereffects of her first real encounter with sexual awareness. Oh, she'd felt stirrings before, the unnamed urges that swept over one at certain times of the month, but never anything like this. Not even that time in college, when sheer curiosity had prompted her to foolhardiness, had she felt anything like this.

Looking at Daniel Avanti had brought on a dizzy breathlessness, like that experienced by the uninitiated in the high altitude of the Alps. And in this, she was uninitiated.

When he stopped in front of her and bent to peer into the back of the car, she felt as if her heart actually stopped for an instant before it shot up to a racing tempo. It pounded even harder, when he spoke.

"Hmm, looks lonely back there. Mind if I ride in front?"

Years of discipline was the only thing that kept Kerith from shouting a denial. While she struggled to form a gracious reply, he went on.

"I know it's irregular, but we're picking up five more guys tonight, and your backseat doesn't look big enough to hold more than that comfortably. Especially if one of them has my long legs." He glanced down at his limbs, and Kerith's eyes automatically followed. Even though dark slacks covered his legs, she could tell they were magnificent, lean and muscular and definitely masculine.

As was the rest of him, she thought, her gaze snagging for a telling microsecond on his fly. Belatedly, she realized what she was doing and jerked her eyes back to his face only to feel the betraying heat of a blush sweep her cheeks. Once again she fell back on professionalism to cover her loss of composure.

"You may sit wherever you wish, Mr. Avanti. I merely thought you'd be more comfortable in the back." She knew *she'd* be a lot more comfortable having him back there.

"I think I'll have a better time up here." Daniel's smile was dazzling as he allowed her to usher him into the front passenger seat. "And I wish you would call me Daniel. It's friendlier."

Kerith thought distractedly, friendlier! That was the last thing she needed right now. In fact, her strongest impulse was to put as much distance as possible between herself and Daniel Avanti's potent charm. Lacking that option, she said with polite determination, "I think Mr. Avanti would be more appropriate. You're paying me to be your chauffeur, not your friend."

"Ah, but I think I'd much prefer having you for a friend," he responded quietly, gazing up at her from the plush interior of the car. All playfulness had vanished from his expression, in its place was a vibrating intensity that had nothing to do with mere friendship. When his dark eyes slowly swept the length of her body, Kerith felt as if summer lightning had suddenly invaded her nervous system. Her first reaction was outrage over his blatant perusal. But then she remembered the embarrassingly long look she'd given him on his porch step, and the urge to put him in his place vanished. After all, she'd started it.

They remained like that for an interminable moment before Daniel finally sighed and broke eye contact. He checked the elegant gold watch that gleamed against the dark hair on his forearm and smiled regretfully. "Unfortunately, I'll have to settle for a chauffeur for now. We're running late and my relatives aren't patient men when it comes to partying."

Kerith let out an inaudible sigh of relief. It was enough just to have the electrifying moment over. She'd analyze her atypical reaction to the man later, when he was a safe distance away. Right now she had a job to do. With a formal little nod, she closed the car door and hurried to take the driver's seat. Unfortunately, she'd never realized before just how intimate the front seat of a limo could be.

2

FROM THE MOMENT Kerith slipped into the driver's seat of the limousine, she began to suspect her sense of relief had been premature. Dusk lent a peaceful, watercolor wash of mauve to the quiet residential streets, but her thoughts were far from tranquil as she skillfully steered the stretch Cadillac toward her second pick-up point. Thanks to years of chauffeuring experience she was able to maintain an outward appearance of calm competence, but inside she struggled against a riot of emotions and sensations, all of them stirred up by the man who now sat only inches away. She'd always scorned the concepts of sensual electricity and instant physical attraction, and having them swoop down on her unaware was demoralizing and a little frightening.

When Daniel turned toward her and spoke, she tensed, preparing to resist yet another round of sensual banter. But he surprised her. "Tell me what it's like to run a limousine service," he requested, drawing her into a completely neutral discussion of their respective businesses. Warmed by relief, she found herself gradually responding to the keen intelligence she soon discovered lurking behind his entrancing dark eyes. He was an adept conversationalist, changing subjects as smoothly as the large automobile changed lanes under Kerith's skilled hands. She'd almost forgotten her original wariness when he shifted into a decidedly personal topic.

"Ali told me you're from Switzerland originally, yet I can barely detect an accent. Have you lived in the States long?"

Kerith's grip on the steering wheel tightened noticeably. How had they gotten from comparing the relative merits of hiring an outside accounting firm to her personal history? Damn Ali. She talked too much.

"I grew up in Switzerland," Kerith admitted reluctantly. "But I attended college in Los Angeles on a scholarship. As for the accent . . . I've always had a knack for that sort of thing. It's the reason I chose languages as my major in college." She threw him a challenging look. "Most people think I was born here."

"I'd probably assume that, too, if it hadn't been for the time I spent in Europe doing liaison work for Uncle Sam." He gave a self-deprecating shrug. "I guess you could say I have a talent for noticing little nuances like that."

If he noticed small details, Kerith didn't want to think about what he'd seen in her response to him. "Exactly what kind of liaison work did you do?" She knew she was breaking her own rule about getting too close to the personal lives of others, but it was better than discussing nuances.

He didn't answer right away, choosing instead to point out the street where his brother-in-law lived. Once Kerith had negotiated the turn, he responded easily. "I was involved in cultural exchange, foreign affairs, that sort of thing. I specialized in sorting out misunderstandings between our government and whoever we happened to be dealing with at the moment. Sort of an international conciliator."

Envisioning him in that role wasn't hard. Kerith would have been willing to bet his incredible charm would work on almost anything that drew breath.

"Now it's your turn," Daniel went on smoothly. "How does a bright, beautiful, multilingual Swiss lady end up owning a limousine service in Sin City?"

It was his second subtle probe for personal information in less than five minutes, and Kerith decided it was time to establish some boundaries. "I doubt you would find the story interesting," she demurred. With an admirable economy of movement, she parked in front of an attractive adobe-styled home.

"On the contrary." Daniel caught her arm as she tried to get out of the car. "I'm completely fascinated."

His large hand was warm where it encircled the soft skin of her upper arm, and it caused an even warmer response in her bloodstream. Even as her body yearned toward that warmth, Kerith forced herself to resist it. She tried to pull away, but he wouldn't release her. "I don't see any need. . . ."

"Come on, Kerith, don't tease me with mysteries." He was using his selling smile again. "They only make me more determined." The gentle, yet firm grip on her arm told her he wasn't bluffing. And since a group of men, obviously the rest of her party for the evening, emerged just then from the house and headed toward the limousine, she decided pacifying him with a little information now would be easier than having him pursue the matter in the company of others.

Letting her irritation show in a huffing sigh, she acquiesced. "I came here with some college friends to celebrate our graduation. They assured me the tab was being picked up by their parents, and when they didn't seem to have any difficulty charging things, I believed them. Then, after three days, my so-called friends disappeared, leaving me with the unpaid bills."

Kerith made a little moue of self-disgust and shrugged. "I needed a job, fast. Fortunately for me, Gus, my late husband, was looking for a chauffeur who could handle the occasional non-English-speaking client. I discovered I really loved the business and stayed. Eventually, Gus and I married, and I inherited the business two years ago when he died. End of story." She looked pointedly at his hand. "Now will you let me go, so I can do my job?"

Daniel nodded slowly, but didn't release her. "Betrayal by a friend, that usually causes some pretty heavy disillusionment," he said thoughtfully. "I hope it hasn't soured you on the idea of friendship." He paused and looked directly into her eyes. "I would never betray you, if you were my friend."

A new kind of alarm shivered to life inside Kerith. Even though she'd purposely delivered her story in an emotionless monotone, this man had immediately zeroed in on the feelings beneath. Coupled with his effect on the rest of her senses, Daniel Avanti's perception was a real threat. In defense, Kerith retreated behind the polite demeanor of an experienced chauffeur. "Thank you for the offer, Mr. Avanti, but I have all the friends I need at the moment."

Daniel saw Kerith's guard go up and knew it was time to let her put a little distance between them. He released her and watched as she left the car to assume her duties with the men outside. Progress had been made, despite her resistance. And while he'd once denounced the attributes that had served Casanova so well, he was gratified to know Kerith wasn't immune to them. Not as a matter of pride, but because of the depth and gathering power of his response to her.

With each smile, each word she uttered, the pull was stronger, drawing him toward feelings and emotions he hadn't experienced in years. It was like being reborn, exhilarating and just a little frightening, given that he still didn't know exactly what Lucretia and her cohorts were up to.

Instinct told him Kerith wasn't an agent, but that only opened up more disturbing possibilities. Maybe she'd had an innocent affair with the wrong person. She might have been involved with an agent from the wrong side, and these powerful friends of hers wanted to make sure she hadn't been converted. He'd handled that sort of case too often. To think of Kerith being involved in such a situation made his gut clench.

Had there been a lover? Perhaps before she left Europe? She would have been young then. Vulnerable. As she'd looked in that second photograph. Daniel's jaw tightened in a barely discernible show of frustration. Lucretia was going to give him some answers, if he had to wring them out of her.

The sound of the rear doors of the limousine opening brought him back to his more immediate goal: the seduction of one reluctant lady in the midst of a stag party for his future brother-in-law. The incongruity of the situation made him smile ruefully.

As KERITH GUIDED the fully loaded limousine through the neon-blazed canyon of the Las Vegas strip, she got a steely grip on herself and vowed to maintain a safe distance from Daniel Avanti for the rest of the evening. No more embarrassingly long looks. No more intimate conversation. She'd just drive the car and keep her eyes on the road.

Daniel, however, wasn't cooperating. While appearing to contribute to the partying in the back of the limo, he managed to maintain a quiet monologue meant for her alone, acquainting her with his boisterous relatives.

There was Frank Bonelli, a lanky, sandy-haired man in western shirt and cowboy boots, who was married to Sophia, the oldest of Daniel's three younger sisters. Jim Peterson, husband to the middle sister, Teresa, was a nuclear physicist at the nearby federal government test site.

Rounding out the party were two cousins, Armand and Tony, and the prospective bridegroom, Dominic Conte, a short, stocky man with a dazzling smile and an epicurean zest for life that sparkled in his dark eyes. Kerith wasn't surprised when Daniel told her Dominic owned Casa del Conte, one of the more elegant Italian restaurants in the city.

By the time she pulled up in front of the sparkling big-top facade of the Circus Circus casino, Kerith felt as if she had somehow been made a part of the close-knit group. But even the mood of easy camaraderie couldn't override the gathering tension in the near seclusion of the plush front seat.

Daniel continued to commandeer the spot next to her as they moved from one glittering establishment to the next, and even the time she spent waiting alone with the limousine wasn't sufficient for her to build any defense against his tantalizing presence. His slightest smile induced the craziest fluttering in her heart, and the deep timbre of his voice wrapped her in sensual warmth even though the conversation was light.

And then there was his scent, a heady mix of expensive after-shave and healthy masculinity that even the air conditioner's cool blast couldn't conquer.

You're imagining it, she told herself for not the first time that evening, as she sat in the waiting area reserved for limousines in front of Caesar's Palace. Caesar's was to be the last stop of the evening, and she eagerly anticipated the moment when she could escape Mr. Daniel Avanti and his dangerous charm. She hadn't felt so threatened, so out of control since the time when Edelweiss dictated her life. And while she'd learned long ago that facing trouble was far more effective than running from it, she'd also discovered sidestepping it entirely was the optimum solution. Yet, here she was toying with the idea of just driving off and leaving her clients to their own devices; a cardinal sin in the chauffeuring business.

She was still worrying the idea like a sore tooth when Daniel and his fellow revelers emerged from the glassed entrance of the casino. Shoving her misgivings aside, Kerith quickly started the limousine and pulled up in front of the gleaming black steps.

Except for Daniel, who appeared as self-possessed as he had when the evening began, they all gave evidence of being well past the legal drinking and driving limit. Shaking her head in amused exasperation, Kerith got out of the car just in time to see Dominic throw back his dark, curly head and burst into a soulful rendition of an Italian aria. She might have laughed if she hadn't noticed one of the doormen begin to signal for the security guards. In a flash, she was up the steps and reaching for the would-be opera star. In the process she nearly collided with Daniel, who'd obviously had the same idea. Even occupied as she was, Kerith reacted to the warm, hard strength of his forearm which rested alongside hers as they hustled Dominic into the waiting limousine.

The others, sensing they'd overstayed their welcome, followed close behind and within minutes were all safely inside, hooting with laughter at their near escape. Kerith didn't waste any time getting under way, but when the car reached the end of the circular drive, Daniel touched her arm lightly, making her hesitate before pulling out into the traffic.

She was coming to expect the little jump in her pulse each time he touched her. What she didn't anticipate was the rush of emotional communion she experienced when their eyes met, a shared glow of accomplishment and relief over their near miss.

"Thanks," he said softly. "That was quick thinking back there. I don't know what my sisters would have done if I'd let any of these clowns get into trouble. Especially Annie, who's going to marry old Pavarotti back there." He jerked his head toward the backseat, then winced as Dominic ran out of Italian lyrics and switched to hilariously ribald English.

A particularly shocking line about tender young maids and lusty men jolted Kerith out of her bemusement. Muttering a quick acknowledgment of his thanks, she turned her attention to the task of merging her long, cumbersome vehicle into the still heavy evening traffic. Dominic continued to serenade them, with the occasional, off-key assistance of the others in the back, and Kerith couldn't resist asking, "Does your sister know what she's getting into?"

"I think she has a fair idea," Daniel replied, his dark eyes sparkling with mirth. "Annie manages his restaurant. Did I tell you he sings while he cooks? Whenever he hears a familiar song on the piped-in music, his patrons are treated to an impromptu concert. He claims they love it."

"Not with those lyrics, I'll bet," Kerith drawled, barely restraining a smile.

"He is rather . . . loose tonight. I think I'd better take him back to my place to sleep it off. Annette will kill me if he's late for the wedding." He spared a glance toward his well-oiled relatives. "You'd better take the others home first, though. I don't want their wives to worry."

By the time they had dropped the others off and returned to Daniel's condo, Dominic had run out of songs and lapsed into snoring slumber. When they couldn't waken him, Kerith had no choice but to help Daniel move the somnolent man inside.

She had a brief impression of comfortable-looking contemporary furnishings in the darkened living room as they half carried Dominic to a long, sectional sofa that formed a U in front of a white brick fireplace. He murmured incoherently as they lowered him onto the ivory cushions, and Kerith was suddenly struck by the potential intimacy of the situation. With Dominic dead to the world, she and Daniel were, for all practical purposes, alone.

With a hastily uttered, "Goodnight, Mr. Avanti. I hope you enjoyed your evening," she turned and nearly ran down the short hallway and out the front door.

Daniel caught up with her on the sidewalk, his large hand encircling her arm at almost the same spot it had held earlier that evening. Kerith's arrested forward momentum pulled her around in a neat arc, and she slammed hard into his big solid body. Reflexively, Daniel wrapped an arm around her waist, steadying her as she stared up at him wide-eyed.

They remained that way for endless, tension-laden moments, and Kerith felt as if she were caught in a still frame of a motion picture, all action suspended except for the rapid pounding of her heart. Daniel's face was so close she could have counted, by moonlight, the heavy midnight lashes that framed his dark eyes. As she watched, his pupils dilated until the irises seemed almost black, and then they were shielded as his lids drooped and his head began to descend.

"Don't." Had that breathless, ineffective protest come from her? She wasn't given time to wonder further. In the next instant Daniel's mouth brushed hers, and it was like lightning touching down on dry desert grass. The flame was so quick, so intense Kerith couldn't think fast enough to fight it. She made a small sound—half gasp, half moan—and immediately felt the wet velvet of

Daniel's tongue slide along her parted lips, teasing, tasting, tempting...

Another moan escaped her, and she felt Daniel's free hand slide under her hair to cup the back of her head and guide her more deeply into his kiss. He didn't plunge or dominate, but rather tempted her with a silken thrust that a more experienced woman would have found irresistible. For Kerith, however, it caused an overload in sensual circuits that had been pushed beyond normal limits all evening. In less than a heartbeat, she was three feet away from him and still backing up. Her golden eyes were enormous, her breasts heaving, her mouth quivering. "Damn you," she whispered raggedly, then turned and ran toward the limousine.

Daniel stood stunned, as much from the unexpected power of that one kiss as from its abrupt end. He realized he hadn't felt that kind of magic in years—if ever. And she hadn't even been kissing him back. Shaking off his amazement, he started after her, then halted when he realized he was too late. Kerith was already in the driver's seat and had the car started.

"Great strategy, Avanti," he muttered disgustedly, as he watched her power away with an inelegant screech of tires. "Spend most the evening trying to impress the lady with your charm and finesse, and then blow it with one, impulsive kiss." He winced as Kerith rounded the first corner with a scream of rubber on pavement. Actually, he hadn't intended to kiss her at all. He'd merely wanted to thank her for filling in for Ali, and for her extra help with Dominic. But the way she'd looked up at him with those sexy golden eyes of hers had driven all thoughts of restraint out of his head.

Casanova never lost control like that. The thought cheered him immeasurably. Casanova rarely felt anything. But Daniel, not Casanova, had agreed to take this assignment. And Daniel was feeling more vitally alive than he had in a long time. As he turned to walk inside he began to whistle softly, his agile mind already plotting how he would smooth things over with Kerith when he saw her the next day at the wedding.

THE FOLLOWING MORNING, tension was high at Classique Limousine's headquarters. More particularly, in Kerith's office.

"Are you positive there isn't anyone else available to drive the Avanti wedding today?" Kerith frowned, and dropped her copy of the weekly scheduling chart onto the wide expanse of her Danish modern desk. The entire office was furnished in the same design, done in satiny white oak, with a cool, turquoise-and-cream color scheme to promote a feeling of discreet elegance.

"I'm positive. I even called all the standbys on our list." Kerith's secretary, Charlotte McAllister shifted on the low chair facing the desk and reached for the discarded schedule. With her free hand, she absently shoved a pencil into her unruly mop of red curls. "You can blame the unseasonably cool temperatures we're having, and the strike in Atlantic City," she added, with a helpless shrug. "Everyone in town, including us, has more business than they know what to do with."

Kerith made a face and bit the end of the gold pen she'd been using to doodle on company stationery.

Delicate edelweiss twined around Classique Limousine's gold-embossed logo, which only served to increase Kerith's ire when she realized what she had been drawing.

"Why don't you want to drive?" Charlotte inquired, confusion clouding her normally cheerful expression. "You're free this afternoon. And you're always telling me how much you love driving the Rolls."

"There isn't a big problem, really," Kerith hedged. Except for a tall, very persistent Italian. "I just . . . had other plans." The most important plan being to avoid Daniel Avanti like the plague. Just the thought of him, sent a rivulet of sensation down her spine. Last night she had lain awake for hours, staring at pale moon shadows on her ceiling, while memories of his strong, hard body and the unique flavor of his mouth painted bright sensual images in her mind. Ultimately, she'd resorted to swimming fast laps in her moonlit pool until exhaustion pulled her into a restless dream-laden sleep.

"Shall I call Mr. Avanti and cancel?" Charlotte offered reluctantly.

Cancel? Kerith's innate business sense balked at the thought. "Of course not. I'll do it, if no one else can." It wouldn't be fair to spoil Annette Avanti's wedding plans just because her brother had dared to kiss his chauffeur last night. She would handle Daniel Avanti somehow. Maybe he wouldn't even remember that kiss today. After all, any man who looked like Daniel probably had women lined up and waiting for his kisses. Not to mention all the other breathtaking activities in which he no doubt excelled.

"Kerith, are you all right? You look a little flushed."

Annoyed at the erotic direction of her musings, Kerith shook her head vehemently. "I'm fine. Just a little tired, after getting in so late last night."

"Well, if you're through with me, I think I'd better get back to typing the schedule for next week." Charlotte hopped up and bustled to the door, then turned back as a last thought struck her. "By the way, when I was refiling some papers in the confidential files this morning, it looked like you'd been searching for something. Did you find it?"

Perplexity, then concern brought Kerith's brows together. Only she and Charlotte had access to the locked file cabinet standing in one corner of Kerith's office. And since Charlotte's filing system tended to be dauntingly precise, Kerith normally let her secretary take care of any record-pulling or refiling that needed to be done. If something looked amiss to Charlotte, there could be cause for concern. Those files held some extremely personal information about Classique's high-class clientele.

Still frowning, Kerith shook her head slowly. "I haven't been in those files since the day you were out sick, a month ago. Are you sure someone other than yourself has been in there?"

Charlotte shrugged, but she was beginning to look uneasy, too. "I could be wrong."

"Nevertheless, I don't like the idea of anyone snooping. Some of our clients are extremely sensitive about their privacy. I think I'll have the combination changed, just to be safe."

"Maybe you should say something about it at the next staff meeting, too. You know, just a casual warning."

"I think I will. And thanks for telling me, even if it is a false alarm."

As Charlotte quietly closed the door behind her, Kerith made a note on her staff-meeting agenda, then did a quick mental inventory of the potentially dangerous information contained in the confidential files.

There were private phone numbers and addresses of at least fifty show-business personalities, and Kerith's notes on the preferences and idiosyncrasies of Classique's regular customers. Such as the married banker who wanted a limousine to meet him at the airport every other month, a well-chilled bottle of Mouton Rothschild and his current show-girl playmate in the backseat. Or the Bible Belt politician who had a weakness for the baccarat tables. Maybe they weren't earth-shattering secrets, but the scandal rags would probably be willing to pay top dollar for some of them.

Kerith also kept most of her personal records in that file cabinet, including the carefully preserved birthday envelopes from Edelweiss, and the stiffly formal letters from the president of the bank in Geneva, politely refusing her repeated pleas for information on her benefactor. Again, not urgent secrets, but things she preferred to keep to herself.

Pressing two fingers to the twin creases between her brows, Kerith sighed wearily and made a note on her calendar to have the cabinet's combination lock changed on Monday. Now, if only there were some way she could as easily rid herself of the other frustrating complications in her life: Edelweiss and Daniel Avanti.

She wasn't any closer to a solution several hours later as she stepped from the private bathroom in her office, dressed once more in her chauffeur's uniform. In fact, she was so busy composing herself for the coming ordeal of facing Daniel Avanti, she didn't notice the blond, arrogantly handsome man lounging against her desk until he spoke.

"My, don't we look stunning today," Arthur Kingston said in his clipped British accent.

Kerith jumped and swung toward him accusingly. "Arthur! You nearly scared me to death. What are you doing in here?"

"Sorry." He smiled guiltily and stood up as she moved toward him. "Charlotte was away from her desk, and I didn't think you'd mind my waiting for you in here."

Kerith realized she was partly to blame for that assumption. For although she maintained a definite personal boundary, beyond which no one was allowed, she encouraged an atmosphere of easy camaraderie among the employees of Classique Limousine, and made a show of joining in it herself. Occasionally it backfired. "Next time, I'd appreciate it if you waited for an invitation to come in."

"Of course. I never meant to overstep," Arthur replied smoothly.

Everything about Arthur was smooth, Kerith thought. His lithe body was shorter than average, but when he was dressed in Classique's distinctive uniform, he exuded an air of sophistication and punctiliousness that made him immensely popular as a chauffeur—especially with women. His thick, fair hair and sharp aristocratic features belied the fifty years he claimed on his employment application. He was also an exemplary employee, always punctual, and willing to work overtime when necessary.

In spite of all that, Kerith couldn't seem to overcome a slight uneasiness whenever she was around him. There was something about Arthur Kingston that just made her edgy. Perhaps it was the occasional hint of cruelty she thought she detected in his cool blue eyes. Or perhaps it was his rather cavalier treatment of the growing number of rich, lonely widows who vied for his attention day and night.

"I tried to call you last night, but you weren't home," he said casually. "Was it, as American teenagers put it, a hot date?" Kerith could feel his eyes on her as she moved to put the comforting width of her desk between them.

Hot date! A lightening-quick memory flared in her brain, of the heat that had swept through her body like wildfire as Daniel kissed her. She quickly ducked her head to head the blaze of color she felt rising to her cheeks. "You might say I had a whole carful," she said with a forced little laugh.

"What?" Arthur sounded slightly outraged.

"I said I had a whole carful of hot dates," she repeated, laughing genuinely when she caught his expression. "I was chauffeuring last night. Ali hurt her foot and couldn't come in."

"Ah! I might have known. Too bad, really. I had tickets to a show at the Flamingo. One of my . . . er, customers had to fly home on short notice and she gave them to me. I thought you and I might go together."

Kerith's eyes narrowed suspiciously. "Trying to add me to your long list of lonely old widows, Arthur?" That was another thing about him that disquieted her—his occasional attempts at elevating their friendly employer-employee relationship to something more personal.

"You wound me, Kerith. I merely wanted to share my good fortune." He leaned one hip on the edge of the desk and picked up the piece of stationery she'd been scribbling on earlier. "You're a talented doodler." He squinted interestedly at the gracefully twined border of edelweiss. "What are these, anyway?"

Quickly plucking the paper from his fingers, Kerith shoved it into a desk drawer and said, "Just flowers. Now, you'll have to excuse me, Arthur. I have a wedding to chauffeur."

"Charlotte mentioned that. Sorry I couldn't take it for you, but I'm booked till two this afternoon. You know I would if I could."

Kerith felt a twinge of guilt. Arthur really could be quite nice at times, in spite of his rather supercilious manner. As recompense for her earlier suspicions, she offered a warm smile. "Thanks, Arthur, I know you would. Want to walk out with me and see the Rolls? I'm using her for the wedding today, and Jamie has been polishing chrome all morning." A self-confessed admirer of Classique's elegant antique, Arthur accepted the invitation with alacrity.

The noon sun poured golden warmth over Kerith's bare forearms and face as she and Arthur crossed Classique Limousine's fenced back lot. Situated in a bustling commercial area west of the Las Vegas strip, the lot had ample room for a modern office building in front, a fair-sized garage in back and plenty of parking space in between for a modest fleet of stretch limousines.

At the moment the parking area was empty, except for the white Cadillac Arthur was due to drive and a majestically beautiful Rolls-Royce Silver Wraith limousine.

Bright sunbeams shimmered along gleaming silver-gray flanks, and sent piercing shards of reflected light off the winged hood ornament. The car's gracefully curved fenders and voluptuously regal silhouette had earned her the nickname "the Duchess" the day Kerith and Gus purchased her at an estate auction. A grand old antique, she personified romance and refinement, even if she did get fractious occasionally.

"Lord, but she's lovely. I just hope she doesn't make trouble for you today," Arthur said, giving voice to Kerith's thought.

"She shouldn't, Mrs. Anders." Jamie unfolded his lanky teenaged frame from where he had been crouched, polishing the car's rear license plate. As Classique's routine maintenance man, he was responsible for keeping the cars sparkling clean and tending to any minor repairs. "Avanti's service manager sent her back last week with a clean bill of health."

"He's done that before," Kerith pointed out with more force than she'd intended. Mere mention of the name Avanti had caused a distressing lurch in her stomach.

"It was pretty bad right after old Joe Avanti died," Jamie conceded with a nod. "But since Daniel took over six months ago, their work has been the best."

"I hope you're right," Arthur put in doubtfully. "Newlyweds generally dislike unscheduled walks." He lifted one hand in a casual salute to Kerith. "I've got to be off now. Good luck with the Rolls. If you get stuck and it's after two, don't hesitate to call."

"Don't worry, Mrs. Anders," Jamie said, as soon as Arthur was safely ensconced in the other limousine. "Even if the Duchess does act up, Daniel will be there to help out."

Don't remind me, Kerith thought dourly. Another quake hit her stomach region, as she got into the car and started the engine. At least the Duchess was behaving so far.

Seeing her frown and misinterpreting its cause, Jamie rushed to reassure her. "Hey, Daniel's really an all-right guy. He even agreed to show me and a couple other guys at Avanti's some basic moves in martial arts. For free!"

"Martial arts?" Kerith echoed disbelievingly. That hardly fit the image of smooth urbanity she'd gotten last night. Although she might have guessed after seeing the fluid, muscular grace of that big body maneuvering in and out of her limousine . . . This time she felt as if her stomach had actually done a double flip.

"He said he picked it up when he was in the Marines," Jamie explained enthusiastically. "He's totally awesome—"

Kerith held up a hand to end what sounded like the beginning of a long diatribe of praise. "All right, I believe you. If the Duchess refuses to start, I'll have him give her a karate chop or something." Jamie laughed and closed the car door, then waved her off with an exaggerated bow.

SAINT ANDREW'S CHURCH was a modern, red-brick structure located in the affluent northwestern section of Las Vegas. Kerith parked the Rolls in front of the sweeping front steps fifteen minutes before the service was due to conclude. After a last-minute check of champagne and glasses, she settled herself comfortably on the pliant leather upholstery of the front seat and prepared to wait. To her annoyance, thoughts of Daniel Avanti immediately popped into her head.

What would he have to say for himself today? Would he try to pick up where they left off last night? Lord, was she ever going to be able to forget that kiss?

Scowling, Kerith fixed her gaze on the church's imposing bell tower, and made herself think about the weather. It was a gorgeous day; sunny, yet lacking the searing heat Las Vegas usually suffered this time of year. A perfect day for a wedding.

She and Gus hadn't been so lucky. A touch of melancholy pressed in on Kerith as she remembered that day, over four years ago. But even unhappy memories were better than thinking about dark-eyed Italians.

The wedding chapel had been small and tawdry, a chilling November rain adding a dank heaviness to the odors of stale cigarette smoke and cheap perfume. Not that she or Gus would have considered a church wedding under the circumstances. Not when they both knew the union would take place on paper only.

Gus, always the gentleman, had put on a good show for the shabby couple who ran the place. His blue eyes had twinkled, as he gave her a bear hug and a gentle buss on the mouth. Only Kerith knew it was more like the caress of a doting father, than a husband.

Oh Gus, why did you have to die?

A dark swarm of old regrets threatened Kerith briefly, but a movement at the front of the church caught her attention just then, breaking the mood. Thoughts of the past faded to insignificance as the large double doors swung outward, and Daniel Avanti stepped into the dazzling sunlight, resplendent in a dove-gray tuxedo. Given the business she was in, Kerith was used to seeing men in tuxedos, but none of them had possessed the breathtaking virility that Daniel brought to formal wear. He'd been potent enough in casual clothing, in a tux he was positively dangerous.

Kerith let out an explosive little sigh, and gathered her resolve as she stepped out of the car. Not one slip, she warned herself. Today she was going to maintain a chauffeur's poise if it killed her. By the time Daniel had loped easily down the stairs, Kerith was waiting on the passenger side of the car, her expression purposefully remote.

"Hello, Kerith." His voice was pitched low, as though he were saying goodnight—from an adjoining pillow! His smile was incandescent.

Kerith gritted her teeth and resisted a reckless urge to smile back. "Good afternoon, Mr. Avanti."

When her eyes remained fixed on the tiny white rosebud nestled against the satin lapel of his jacket,

Daniel bent down until they were almost nose to nose. He looked surprisingly abashed. "I guess you're still angry with me for kissing you last night, hmm?" His dark brows arched appealingly, as he let out a regretful sigh. "I'm really sorry I upset you. Normally, I make sure my attentions will be welcomed before proceeding. Last night I just seemed to lose my head." An amazingly boyish grin creased his handsome face. "I don't suppose you'd be willing to make allowances, if I told you I have a terrible weakness for women in uniform?"

Amusement and embarrassment warred for supremacy behind Kerith's carefully composed expression. She didn't want to remember that kiss, damn it. And while she knew she should acknowledge his apology as impersonally as possible, she was sorely tempted to grin back at him and give in to that wonderful charm. Common sense prevailed only when she happened to glance at the entrance to the church. "No allowances are necessary, Mr. Avanti. Consider the incident forgotten. Now, if you'll excuse me, I think the wedding party is about to descend upon us. And there's a pretty blond lady in a bridesmaid dress who's standing at the top of the steps glaring at you."

Daniel's gaze followed hers to the gaily dressed crowd spilling from the church doors and fanning out on the wide steps. Poised in the doorway, ready to make their dash through a shower of rice, were the bride and groom. When he spotted the scowling young woman in pink satin, who stood next to them, he groaned. "That's Claudia, the maid of honor. She thinks my being best man means I should be glued to her side for the day."

Kerith managed a nonchalant shrug and opened the rear door of the limousine. "Why are you complaining? She's very attractive."

Daniel braced an arm on top of the open door and watched her pull an icy bottle of champagne from the tiny refrigerator located in the back. "I told you," he said, as she straightened and began to uncork the bottle with unstudied skill. "I have a thing for women in uniform. Especially ones who fill them out the way you do."

Kerith nearly dropped the bottle of champagne, as tingling, electric heat zapped through her body, just as it had the night before when he'd so blatantly charted her physical assets with his eyes. She was trying to formulate a properly discouraging reply, when the newlyweds arrived at the bottom of the steps—breathless and laughing amidst a shower of rice—and the opportunity was gone.

For the next few minutes, Kerith had her hands full getting them settled in the back of the Rolls with glasses of complimentary champagne. She was only peripherally aware when Daniel sprinted back up the church steps. She did, however, have time to note that Daniel's sister Annette possessed a feminine version of her brother's stunning attractiveness.

Daniel reappeared, escorting a now-beaming Claudia, and he gallantly helped her onto one of the rear jump seats that folded down to accommodate extra passengers. Kerith was about to circle the car and offer him the adjacent jump seat, when something small and solid barreled into the back of her legs, tumbling her right into Daniel's arms. She stiffened immediately, half expecting him to take advantage of the situation. Instead, he acted the perfect gentleman, swiftly setting her upright almost before anyone could notice, using only one strong hand on her shoulder to steady her. When he spoke, his voice conveyed genuine concern. "Are you all right?"

Slightly dazed, Kerith nodded, while a funny glow blossomed in the region of her heart. Was it possible he sensed her abhorrence of losing her composure in front of others? "I . . . I think so. What hit me?"

"A pint-sized tornado, I'm afraid." Daniel smiled ruefully and nodded toward a small boy who was bouncing around them like a jet-propelled pogo stick. "Meet my nephew, Joey Peterson." He placed a calming hand on Joey's head. "Slow down, pal. I think you owe this lady an apology."

"Sorry, Mrs. . . .lady," came the sheepish response. The child was a darling, miniature version of his uncle, right down to his gray tuxedo and entrancing dark eyes. And when he raised those eyes to Kerith and pleaded for a ride in the Rolls, she began to wonder if all Avanti males were gifted with the ability to charm a woman's socks off with a single look. Of course, she agreed to let him ride.

"And you can call me Kerith," she added, helping him into the front seat. "Mrs. Lady seems a little formal."

"So you're a softy when it comes to kids," Daniel mused quietly, from behind her. "Perhaps I should have Joey plead my case the next time I kiss you."

The outrageous presumption of his calm statement touched off an automatic rebellion in Kerith. How dare he assume there would be a next time? Completely forgetting her resolve to maintain a professional demeanor, she turned and fixed him with a cool stare. "There's a name for people who use other people to gain what they want. It's manipulator. And I think you should know, I have no tolerance for them."

For several seconds Daniel appeared too surprised to respond. Then, when he did speak, there was an odd note of regret in his voice. "In view of that, I think there's something I'd better confess now . . ." he began, only to be interrupted by Dominic's voice coming from the interior of the limousine.

"Hey, Daniel, could you romance the chauffeur later? I'd like to get to my wedding reception before I celebrate my first anniversary."

There was a rifle of laughter from the small crowd gathered around the limousine, and Kerith wished that the earth would open and swallow her whole. Mortified beyond words, she gave Daniel a fulminating glare, then marched around the car to wait pointedly by the rear passenger door. He followed promptly enough, but before taking the remaining jump seat, he leaned close and whispered for her ears only, "I intend to finish this conversation at the first opportunity."

Not if I have anything to say about it, Kerith swore silently as she buckled herself into the driver's seat. But then another thought distracted her from her fury. *Confess?* What in the world had he intended to confess?

3

THE RIDE TO DOMINIC'S restaurant, where the wedding feast was to be held, should have been routine for Kerith, even considering the dozen cars that followed the limousine, honking wildly, and the steady stream of questions that poured from little Joey. Such things were only minor distractions to a seasoned chauffeur, yet when she finally pulled up in front of the white, Moorish-style building housing Casa del Conte, Kerith was hard-pressed to restrain a sigh of relief.

Having Daniel seated behind her and out of sight had in no way diminished Kerith's awareness of him. And even though Claudia brazenly attempted to monopolize his attention throughout the trip, each time Kerith glanced at the rearview mirror, she encountered the reflection of his dark, penetrating gaze. Confess? What could he possibly have to confess to her?

A large crowd of family and friends had gathered outside the restaurant, and they flowed forward in a warm familial wave, encompassing first the bride and groom, then Daniel and Claudia as they emerged from the back of the limousine.

Kerith helped Joey get out and tried to ignore the affectionate interplay; a discipline she'd learned as a child. There was no point in hungering after things you couldn't have. But for some reason her eyes kept returning to the happy crowd, where kisses and hugs were being exchanged with abandon. And as she watched Daniel bend to embrace an elderly woman whose smile matched his exactly, Kerith couldn't deny a twinge of curiosity.

How would it feel to be surrounded by people who had known you all your life; who had known your parents before you were born, and maybe their parents before them? What would it be like to know where you'd gotten your eye and hair color, your smile, or even your name?

A hollow ache began to spread in Kerith's stomach, and she closed her eyes briefly to fight it off. Self-pity was a wasted emotion. Years ago she'd come to understand there were some things she would never know, including the kinds of things a man like Daniel Avanti represented.

"Hey Kerith, are you okay? You look kinda sad."

Startled out of her silent reflection, Kerith looked down and found Daniel's nephew regarding her with a worried look on his cherubic face. "I'm fine, Joey," she murmured, embarrassed that he had witnessed her un-characteristic self-indulgence. So much of her behav-ior had been out of the ordinary since she had met Daniel Avanti. The man posed a real threat to the care-fully schooled thought processes that had protected her for years.

"You don't look fine," Joey insisted, his big brown eyes solemnly searching her face. "You look like you need a hug."

The idea surprised her into a smile. Hunching down until they were eye-to-eye, she chucked his soft babyish chin. "A hug, hmm? Sounds nice. Do you happen to have one you could spare?"

Joey's answering smile was adorably gap-toothed.

He was going to be a real lady-killer when he grew up, Kerith thought. Just like his uncle. Still smiling, she gathered his sturdy little body into her arms. Joey hugged with an almost fierce affection that brought a stinging pressure of tears against the back of her eyes. How long had it been since she'd allowed herself this kind of closeness with anyone? Holding, being held like this, how sweet it was—so achingly sweet. If only the price weren't so high . . .

Joey's small grunt of protest gusted against her ear, making Kerith realize her grip had grown too tight. She released him and smiled apologetically. "Sorry if I squeezed too hard. I haven't had much practice lately."

"That's okay. Uncle Daniel used to do that, too, when he first came back. Mommy said it was because he was so happy to be with us again, but I saw tears in his eyes sometimes. Just like you have now."

Kerith blinked hard against the telltale moisture and tried not to show her dismay. "Well, sometimes tears can be happy. Did you know that?"

"I guess so." Joey shrugged and stuffed his small fists in the pockets of his trousers. He studied her soberly for a moment, then his expression lightened, as if a happier idea had just occurred to him. "Would you like to get married, Kerith?"

Suppressing amusement as his abrupt change of subject, Kerith pretended to consider him seriously. "I'm not sure. Are you proposing?"

Joey chortled and scuffed one small black shoe on the pavement. "Nah, not me. I'm never gonna get married. But Mommy and Gramma Rosa say Uncle Daniel needs a wife, and I think you'd be a nice one."

This time she couldn't hold back her laughter, but it quickly died when an all-too-familiar male voice sounded behind her. "Good grief, sport, have they stooped to using you as a matchmaker now?"

With a silent curse against the unrelenting force of fate that seemed bent on putting her at a disadvantage with Daniel Avanti, Kerith rose slowly and met his twinkling gaze.

"Although I have to admit, Joey," he continued smoothly, "you have better taste in women than your mother and grandmother. What do you say, Kerith? Will you marry me?"

The outrageously casual way he said it—like a man requesting a luncheon date—gave Kerith an equally outrageous urge to laugh and say yes, just to see what he'd do. But instead she pulled a stern face and said, "I'm afraid not, Mr. Avanti. My chauffeurs aren't allowed to accept proposals of any kind while on duty."

"Well, then, at least say you'll come inside and help me celebrate my sister's marriage."

"You can't tell him that's against the rules," a husky feminine voice chimed in.

Kerith swung around and frowned suspiciously at the stunning brunette who was strolling toward them, leaning gracefully on the arm of a tanned, athletic-looking man. "Ali! What are you doing here? You're supposed to be home nursing a sprained ankle."

Ali's former years as a show girl were manifested in the dramatically pained smile she offered before responding. "I don't suppose you'd buy the idea of a miracle cure?"

"Dammit, Ali. I told you to wait until I could explain." Daniel stepped forward, positioning himself between the two women.

Like a referee in a fight, Kerith thought, her suspicions growing by leaps and bounds. Daniel's earlier need to confess came back to her with distressing implications.

"I know what you said." Ali shrugged impatiently. "But I discovered I have no taste for deceiving my friends. And besides, I hate skulking around." Her green eyes were imploring when she turned her gaze on Kerith. "I know it was a rotten thing to do, but I faked the sprained ankle so you'd have to chauffeur and you and Daniel would have a chance to meet. Given your normal reaction to meeting any of my male friends, it seemed like the only way. I even tried to call you and warn you last night, but you were already gone."

Ali's male companion, who had been listening with the bored incomprehension of a career jock, suddenly lit up. "You mean you had her chauffeur this guy on her own blind date? Out'a sight!"

Kerith spared him a scornful glance before fixing Ali with a look that should have set fire to her elegant, green silk dress. Greater fury than she'd ever known simmered in her veins, made worse by the underlying hurt of Ali's breach of faith. When she spoke, her voice vibrated with quiet accusation. "I thought you were my friend."

Ali flinched as if from a physical blow, then paled as she began to comprehend the extent of Kerith's wrath. "I was . . . I am. . . . Oh damn, I never dreamed you'd be this upset."

Upset? That doesn't begin to describe it, Kerith wanted to scream. But of course she didn't. Public displays of temper were unthinkable to her. So she contented herself with saying tightly, "I ought to leave right now and let you explain to the bride and groom why they won't be riding in the Rolls to their honeymoon retreat. I won't, however, because I assume they knew nothing about this little subterfuge. As for your part in it, Ali, we'll discuss it in my office tomorrow morning. Seven-thirty, sharp!"

As she walked away from the small stunned group, Kerith heard Ali's horrified whisper, "I think she's mad enough to fire me."

And Daniel's murmured response. "Let me handle it, Ali. I'm the one to blame. After all, I talked you into it."

A grim sort of satisfaction settled over Kerith as she circled to the driver's side of the Rolls. Firing Ali hadn't occurred to her up to that point, and even if it had, she wouldn't have seriously considered it. She wasn't the kind of employer who used the threat of dismissal to exact top performance from her employees, and she never used it to solve personal differences, unless the employees in question had performance problems, also. Still, it would serve Ali right to let her stew about it for a while. Maybe she wouldn't be so eager to play matchmaker next time.

She was reaching for the door handle when Daniel stopped her. "Kerith, I need to talk to you."

'H ven't you caused enough damage for one day?" She tried again for the door, but he put his hand on her shoulder, turning her until her back was pressed to the sun-warmed metal.

"Damage?" His eyebrows rose inquiringly. "Isn't that a little strong? I admit Ali and I shouldn't have lied to you about the ankle, but what actual damage has been done?"

"How about betrayal of a friendship?"

Daniel sighed impatiently. "I find it hard to look at it that way, when I know Ali was only trying to do something nice for two of her friends. And last night was very nice," he added with an intimate smile. "If you're honest, I think you'll admit you enjoyed it just as much as I did." When she didn't respond, he put one finger under her chin and tilted it up until she had to look directly at him. "Come on, look me right in the eye and tell me you didn't enjoy it."

Kerith fully intended to resist him, to jerk her head away, stamp her foot down on his highly polished dress shoe, or at least avoid looking into his eyes. But the deep, soothing cadence of his voice was having a decidedly calming effect on her fury, and when she encountered those meltingly dark brown eyes, all she could think about was the bedazzling fire of a moonlit kiss. "I thought we agreed to forget about . . . that," she said with as much steel as she could muster.

Daniel's smile broadened. "I was referring to the conversation and the company, but now that you mention it, the kiss was pretty spectacular. So are you. Can you blame a man for going to any lengths to have a little of your time?" His mouth tilted in wry humor.

"Even when it means being chaperoned by five of his drunken relatives?"

"I told you how I feel about manipulators," Kerith said, stubbornly clinging to the remnants of her resistance. "Justifying what you did doesn't change the fact that you and Ali lied to me."

"Does that mean you're thinking of firing her?" His hands gripped her shoulders with sudden earnestness. "Please don't. I'm the one who's really responsible. Be angry with me if you must, but don't punish Ali for something I talked her into." Daniel might have argued further, but Claudia chose that moment to swoop down on them in a huff. "Daniel! For heaven's sake, will you come on? The photographer has everyone lined up for pictures inside and you're the only one missing."

Annoyance creased Daniel's features for a moment, but then he favored the scowling young woman with a heart-melting smile. "Tell them I'll be along in a minute, will you, love? I need to clear something with the chauffeur." Claudia hesitated, her blue eyes narrowing a bit suspiciously at the way Daniel's hands rested on Kerith's shoulders, but in the end she gave in and even smiled as she left to do his bidding.

As they watched Claudia swish away in her long skirts, Kerith couldn't resist commenting. "Did you take a course on calming irate women, or were you born with the talent?"

Daniel's soft laughter caressed her senses. "Did I calm you? Good. Maybe Ali won't have to go job-hunting after all."

"I never said I was going to fire her," Kerith retorted, shrugging out of his grasp. He was standing too close again; so close she could smell the delicate white rose-bud pinned to his lapel, its fragile perfume in startling counterpoint to the more potent essence of the man towering over her. It reminded her sharply of her own vulnerability to him.

"Just because I'm calmer, doesn't mean I'm not angry with you," she said, giving him a challenging look.

"Yes, but you won't stay angry," Daniel answered softly. "Because under that cool exterior of yours beats a warm, generous heart. I saw it first with Dominic, then with little Joey today. That attracts me to you even more than the memory of how sweet your mouth tastes. It makes me want to—" He didn't get a chance to finish, because another voice hailed him from the direction of the restaurant.

"Daniel! For Pete's sake, if you have to flirt with the chauffeur, could you at least bring her inside to do it?" The speaker was a petite, auburn-haired young woman, with a rounded, obviously pregnant tummy, and she was waiting impatiently by the restaurant's open door.

Daniel glanced toward her and swore softly. "That's my sister Teresa. I suppose my mother will be out next."

The spark of humor in his eyes indicated he wasn't really concerned about the possibility, but Kerith was horrified. She pushed hard against his ruffled, white shirtfront forcing him several steps back. "Damn you, Daniel Avanti. Do you have any idea what you're doing to my business image?"

Daniel sighed. "Does that mean you won't come inside?"

"Absolutely!" Kerith's temper was back in full force, fueled by a blaze of embarrassment.

"All right, I'll go. But I haven't given up on you. You'll be hearing from me soon. Count on it!" With those provocative words, he made his exit, heading toward his waiting sister. Halfway there he turned around and continued his progress backward long enough to offer Kerith a parting shot. "By the way, I love it when you call me Daniel, but you really should drop the 'damn.'"

The door of the Rolls took the brunt of Kerith's anger when she slammed it shut behind her seconds later. "Damn Daniel Avanti, that's a good name for him," she muttered wrathfully as she scanned the parking lot for a place large enough to hold the Rolls. Leaving it on the street was asking for trouble, and she had more than enough of that at the moment. She was further incensed when she tried to get the key in the ignition, and discovered her hands were shaking too hard to manage the simple task.

What was happening to her? Lately it seemed as though there was a conspiracy against the calm, safe world she had built for herself. First there had been the emotional bombshell of Edelweiss's possible reentry into her life. That alone might not have been enough to undermine her poise. But then Ali had to drag Damn Daniel Avanti into the picture, and things had been going downhill ever since. Even her own body was betraying her. How was it possible for her pulse to be altered by the mere presence of a man? And how could the mere mention of a kiss send pleasure winging through her like a herd of sun-drunk butterflies?

"What's it going to be next?" she groused, finally getting the key inserted. When she turned it, however, her reward was complete silence. She turned it again. And again. Nothing. Not even a click.

Letting her head drop forward against the steering wheel, Kerith groaned wearily, "*Et tu*, Duchess?"

She'd have to call a towing service. Visions of wading through the mob of Avantis inside the restaurant, or worse yet, having to ask Daniel for help, made her groan again. But after a moment her head snapped up defiantly. She'd be damned before she went into that restaurant. There were other phones in the businesses nearby. She'd use one of them, have the car towed, and get out of here without Daniel ever knowing about it. One of the other drivers—perhaps Arthur—could take care of the rest of this ride. Fate might be trying to throw her another curve, but that didn't mean she had to meekly accept it. She'd been taking care of herself for a long time now. She didn't need anyone. Not Daniel, not Edelweiss, not anyone!

THE EMPLOYEE LOUNGE at Classique Limousine was deserted when Kerith entered it on Monday morning. Only the mechanical hum of the compact refrigerator greeted her as she skirted the comfortable couch and chairs grouped around a small television set, and headed toward the counter spanning one end of the room. The counter held a microwave oven and automatic coffee maker, the latter of which lured her with the irresistible aroma of freshly brewed coffee. Today she needed the caffeine as much as the rich flavor. It wasn't easy to get up in the morning when one spent half the night in a pool trying to work off a restlessness that seemed to worsen with every hour. She refused to even think about the cause.

"Sneaking in for an early caffeine fix, huh?" Ali's voice came unexpectedly from the door, causing Kerith to jump and spill her coffee.

"Good grief, you scared me." Scowling, Kerith grabbed a paper towel and blotted the hot liquid.

"Sorry." Ali's classic features tightened into a grimace of regret as she came into the room, a hanger bearing her chauffeur's uniform slung over one shoulder. "And while I'm at it, I'd like to apologize again for the other business. I know there's no excuse for lying, but when Daniel told me how he'd seen you once when you picked up one of the limos at his garage, and how he hadn't been able to get you off his mind . . . Well, I just couldn't resist getting the two of you together somehow."

Kerith's scowl deepened, and Ali lifted her hands beseechingly. "I meant well. Look, Daniel hasn't shown much interest in women since he moved back here, and his family is getting concerned. They're hoping he'll settle down with a family of his own soon." Ali smiled ruefully as she helped herself to the coffee. "And since he's thirty-eight and never been married, I suppose they're entitled to worry. When he started raving about you, it seemed almost providential."

"I'm not the answer to their prayers. I'm allergic to familial ties."

"What about me and my daughter? At times, I think Cami actually forgets you're not really her aunt. And I've come to think of you as one of the family, too, especially after all the good times we had together." Ali reached to touch Kerith's arm tentatively. "I'd hoped you felt the same way. Please tell me I haven't ruined things with this business about Daniel. I think I'd rather be fired than lose your friendship."

Kerith shifted uncomfortably and busied herself straightening a stack of napkins. She had spent a lot of time with Ali and her adorable eight-year-old daughter since Gus died, although she'd never thought of it in Ali's terms. The question now was, did she want to continue the relationship, with all its inherent risk of emotional involvement, or should she back away?

For that matter, could she back away? This was Ali, the woman who'd shared the lonely vigil in Gus's hospital room the night he died. The one who had seen to it that Kerith had eaten and rested in the difficult weeks after his death. Ali was right, they had formed a sort of surrogate family. What must be decided now was, should it continue?

Kerith frowned and stared into the steaming, dark liquid in her mug. She should say no. What Ali was asking went against every self-protective instinct Kerith possessed. But when she turned and saw tears shimmering in Ali's sea-green eyes, the decision was made.

"You and Cami do mean a lot to me," Kerith conceded slowly. "But I'm going to need some time to forget this incident. In addition, you'll have to swear on your sweet daughter's life that you'll give up trying to arrange my social life."

Relief flooded Ali's expression and tears spilled over onto her cheeks. "I swear!"

Kerith pulled some tissues from a nearby box and handed them over. "You'd better go get yourself together. It's time for work."

"Thanks, Kerith. You won't regret it." Her smile was tremulous, but her step was jaunty as she headed for the changing rooms.

On the way back to her office, Kerith experienced a strange elation. She'd done the right thing, giving Ali another chance. Allowing one friendship to deepen didn't mean she was relinquishing all control of her life. As far as she was concerned the episode with Daniel Avanti was over now. And if he showed signs of pursuing the matter, she'd put him off as easily and effectively as she did other men.

That opportunity came sooner than she expected. Kerith had barely settled herself in the soft, cream leather of her executive chair, when Charlotte buzzed on the intercom to announce a call from Mr. Avanti on line two.

"Just my luck, he's the persistent type," she muttered to herself, glaring at the insistently flashing button on her telephone. Well, he wasn't going to get the best of her this morning. She punched the button and said with distant politeness, "This is Mrs. Anders. How may I help you, Mr. Avanti?"

There was a significant pause and then his deep, compelling voice came, stroking her senses to instant, tingling awareness. "It's Daniel, remember? Why did you run away yesterday?"

A sudden breathlessness caught Kerith unaware. Damn the man and his sexy voice. "What . . . what are you talking about?" she managed finally.

"The Rolls. It and you were gone when I stepped out to check on you yesterday, and some stiff-upper-lip British type was there to replace you. Then, when I came to work this morning, I found the Rolls sitting in my shop. When I questioned the tow driver, he said he'd picked it up in front of Dominic's restaurant Saturday. Why didn't you come in and ask for help?"

Drawing a steadying breath, Kerith said, "I had no desire to see either you or Ali again."

Daniel sighed regretfully. "Have you seen her yet today?"

"Yes, and I think we've managed to salvage our friendship, no thanks to you."

"I guess I deserve that. What can I do to redeem myself in your eyes?"

"Try leaving me alone," she replied promptly, then quietly hung up on him.

DANIEL SAT BACK, propped his feet on his desk and regarded the dead telephone receiver with disgust. *Well, you certainly handled that well. You must be losing your touch, Casanova, old boy.* How ironic that it should happen with the first woman he'd really cared about in years. Lucretia would die laughing if she knew. As it was she'd nearly crowed with triumph when he called her last night.

"I knew you'd come around, Casanova," she gloated. "Is the grease-monkey business beginning to pall?"

"Not at all. This is a one-time offer. I'm only doing it out of consideration for a valued business associate." If he had anything to say about it, Lucretia would never know of his rapidly deepening personal involvement with Kerith. "In addition, I'm running the show," he added firmly. "I don't want any more of your snoops nosing around the lady. I'll tell you whatever you need to know. I also want more information on the people behind all this, including a motive."

Lucretia hadn't been overjoyed by those terms, but when she found out he'd already made contact with Kerith, she didn't have much choice. "All right, you're running the show, within reason," she agreed reluctantly. "As for the details you're demanding, I'm afraid I don't have that much. I do know that the meeting with Kerith has been requested by Edelweiss, the former benefactor mentioned in her dossier. And that Kerith shouldn't be told anything until she's contacted by Edelweiss."

"Just a quiet little reunion, hmm?" Daniel laughed mirthlessly. "Come on, Lucretia, that doesn't sound likely, given the kind of money they're offering."

Lucretia's sigh was eloquent, even over the miles of long distance line. "You were never this suspicious when you worked for me before."

"I wasn't as smart, either."

"All right, there is a slight complication. Apparently, Edelweiss has a superior who's a stickler for security. He wants one of our people around as insurance against any embarrassing international incidents, and he's willing to pay well for that insurance."

"Good Lord, you mean Edelweiss is one of their agents?"

"Retired agent, actually. But still quite important to them. These people are big-time, Casanova. When they want something, we normally don't ask for detailed reasons why."

Daniel had been inclined to withdraw from the whole mess at that point, but something had held him back. Perhaps it was the memory of that look Kerith got in her eyes at times. When she was watching the loving interactions of his family, for instance, or when she thought she'd been betrayed by Ali. The soul-wrenching power of that look didn't diminish with remembering. Like it or not, he had to see the thing through. Lucretia had sounded triumphant when she hung up.

The receiver in Daniel's hand began to beep its off-the-hook warning, reminding him of the call Kerith had just ended so abruptly. Leaning forward, he hung up the phone and slumped back again. Now what?

Fingers steepled on his flat stomach, he toyed with several possibilities, all of which he discarded on the basis they would most likely spook Kerith irreparably. Maybe it was time for a little old-fashioned wooing. Flowers, candy, the works. Yeah, that just might be the ticket. A new spark of resolve lit his dark eyes as he reached for the phone once more.

KERITH SHOULD HAVE had no problem keeping Daniel Avanti out of her thoughts. She certainly had enough business to keep her mind fully occupied during the rest of the day. There were schedules to review, contracts to consider, calls to return, and in between it all, she interviewed several people who wished to train as chauffeurs. She didn't have time to think about Daniel, but that didn't seem to matter.

The harder she tried to concentrate, the clearer became the disturbingly alluring vision of his handsome face. It superimposed itself on paperwork and walls and once, embarrassingly enough, on the face of one of her male chauffeurs. Chagrin had given her cheekbones a warm apricot color when she caught the poor man's guarded look, and realized she'd been staring at him distractedly instead of answering his question.

Matters didn't improve at all when the flowers arrived mid-afternoon. Roses. Masses and masses of pale apricot buds, whose nectar-sweet fragrance filled her office, not to mention her head. The enclosed card had read:

> Their color reminded me of your lovely blushes, but their scent isn't half as enticing as yours. Forgive me. Aside from everything else, I'd like to be your friend.
>
> Daniel

His words caused a strange stirring in her soul, and she knew she must put a quick end to this new approach. But when she called his office, fully intending to politely thank him for the flowers, and just as politely refuse his offer of friendship, his secretary told her Mr. Avanti was away on business for the rest of the day. Kerith suppressed a groan of frustration and declined to leave a message.

By the time she arrived home that evening she felt tense and irritable from the daylong struggle to keep her mind off Daniel Avanti. Dinner would have to wait, she decided, stripping as she headed for the bedroom.

Within ten minutes she was doing rhythmic laps, the pool's refreshing water flowing over her naked body like a lover's caress, or rather what she imagined a lover's caress to be. Floodlights turned the pool's surface to rippling silver in the gathering twilight.

At the end of a particularly long underwater run, she surfaced to the sound of the phone ringing. Unsure of how many rings she'd missed, Kerith lunged out of the pool and grabbed the receiver. Her "hello" was understandably breathless, but her breath caught and held when she heard a familiar bass voice greet her.

"Hello, Kerith. It's Daniel. Did I interrupt your bath?"

"What makes you think I was taking a bath?" she demanded tartly, hoping he couldn't hear the betraying tremor in her voice.

"You took quite a while to answer the phone . . . and you sound wet and naked."

Kerith sucked in a shocked breath, and glanced down at herself. Her nipples had contracted until they looked like dusky little buds against her golden tan, and a heavy warmth seemed to swell in her breasts.

After a long, telling moment, Daniel's breath hissed in, too. "Sweet heaven, you really are, aren't you? I knew I should have dropped by unannounced."

His last words were light, teasing, but there was an undertone of raw desire that jolted Kerith's defense system back to working order. "How did you get my home number? It's unlisted, and Ali swore she wouldn't interfere anymore."

"You forgot, we're business associates. I have it on file at work," he replied smoothly. "I also know where you live."

Kerith shivered and hastily reached for her robe. "Is that some kind of threat?"

Daniel's husky laughter filled her ear. It was, she decided, the kind of sound that could dissolve even the stiffest backbone, and hers had been in a steady decline since she'd first met this man.

"I never threaten, I coax," he said softly.

"Then why did you call?" She had the robe on now, and some of her self-possession was returning.

"I was going to ask you that. My secretary said you called today, and gave your name but no message."

"Oh, that. I just wanted to thank you for the roses. Which, by the way, you shouldn't have sent. I thought I made myself clear, I'm not interested."

"You sound different. Did you put something on?"

This time his perception made her angry. "Damn it, if you don't stop talking so...so suggestively, I'm going to hang up on you."

"Please don't. At least not until you agree to have dinner with me tomorrow."

"Not a chance."

"Lunch then."

"I'm busy."

"We need to discuss the ills of your beloved Duchess."

Mention of the Rolls made Kerith sit down abruptly on the nearest chaise lounge. "What about the Duchess?"

"Uh-uh. Not over the phone. I'll see you at noon, to-morrow. Lunch is on me."

"No! Wait. . . ." She was addressing a dead line.

THE FOLLOWING MORNING another gift from Daniel ar-rived at Classique Limousine. To make matters worse, the special messenger showed up right in the middle of the weekly personnel meeting, and the large gold-foil package he handed over caused a storm of speculation among Kerith's employees. She gave in gracefully to their pleas that she unwrap the box, and even passed it around to let them sample the expensive Swiss choco-lates within, but the enclosed card she slipped into the pocket of her white linen blazer. No telling what Dan-iel had written this time.

Later, in the safety of her office she read his bold script:

They say chocolate is a sensuous food. Will you think of me each time one of these melts against your tongue?

Your friend,
Daniel

Something elemental shivered through Kerith, and it wasn't a craving for chocolate. How had he known of her utter weakness for that particular brand? And how could she possibly sit across from him at lunch, and calmly discuss the mechanical problems of the Rolls after reading that note?

The latter question hovered on the back of her con-sciousness like a half-finished melody as she moved through her routine morning business, which included several long-distance calls to arrange the final details on limousine service for upcoming conventions. She still didn't have an answer when Charlotte buzzed on the intercom to announce in a slightly giddy voice that a Mr. Avanti was there to see her.

Kerith barely had time to stand up and brace herself against her desk, before Daniel strolled in, looking cool and inordinately virile in a beige, summer-weight suit. Her senses started overreacting immediately, and she tried to compensate with drollery. "Do you always carry a purse for business lunches?" she inquired, her eyes dropping to the large wicker basket slung over his left arm.

"Always." Daniel grinned and winked at Charlotte, who returned his smile dreamily and left, pulling the door firmly shut behind her. "Nice secretary," he said, scanning the office with undisguised interest. "She was most helpful when I called about the flowers and candy."

"So that's how you found out. I'm going to have to do something about the spies in my ranks . . . What are you doing?"

Daniel looked up from spreading a red-checked cloth on the low coffee table positioned under one of the office's large, tinted glass windows. "I thought a picnic would be nice, and since you're not exactly dressed for the park . . ." His eyes moved admiringly over her white, pleated skirt and peach silk blouse. "Not that I'm complaining."

Kerith started to protest, then reconsidered. Maybe she would be better off here, with familiar surroundings to remind her of who she was, and why she shouldn't respond to this man. She watched in bemusement as Daniel's beige jacket and brown silk tie landed on a chair. And then he was striding toward her purposefully, rolling up the sleeves of his crisp yellow shirt as he came.

"But a picnic in an office?" she asked vaguely, her attention caught by strong forearms lightly brushed with black hair. "You must be crazy."

"Only about you." Daniel gave her one of his special smiles as he led her to the impromptu picnic area and settled her on the thickly carpeted floor.

"But why? I keep telling you I'm not interested. A man like you could probably have his pick of women any day of the week. Why bother with me?"

Daniel had eased down next to her, and now he leaned closer on one arm. "Because," he said, his gaze resting on her mouth for a moment, then lifting to delve deep into her eyes. "You're the first woman I've really wanted in over seventeen years."

Kerith burst into incredulous laughter. "Oh, come on. You expect me to believe you've never..." Realizing what she'd been about to say, she bit her lip and looked away. How did they get on this subject so quickly?

Daniel smiled and touched a blunt fingertip to the blush warming her cheekbones. "You're confusing wanting with lust. Wanting involves what's in here." He moved his fingertip to her temple, then trailed it down to the peach silk covering her left breast. Beneath it her heart pounded with a new, reckless rhythm. "And here." His eyes roved slowly downward and back up. "In addition to all the rest."

She felt certain he was going to kiss her then, but he surprised her by turning to the basket and busying himself with pouring a glass of chilled, sparkling mineral water for each of them. After slipping a slice of lemon into one crystal goblet, he handed it to her.

"I've only felt this way once before," he continued after a sip of his drink. "And that was a long time ago, with a girl named Angelina." One corner of Daniel's attractive mouth quirked with bitterness. "Unfortunately, my family felt she wasn't good enough for me."

The implications of what he had said startled Kerith into blunt inquisitiveness. "You mean they actually forbade you to see her? I didn't think families could do that anymore in the free world."

Daniel smiled sadly. "You obviously haven't had much contact with old-fashioned Italian families. My father wasn't a harsh man, really, just immovable when he thought he was right. He vowed to disown me if I married Angelina. Not that that would have stopped me, if things hadn't been taken out of my hands." Daniel shifted restlessly and began rummaging around in the basket again. "Here we are. Croissants with crab salad and crudités with herbed yogurt. Your favorites, according to Charlotte."

Kerith opened the packages of food he placed before her on the table, and they ate in silence for a few minutes. But she couldn't focus on eating, not without knowing what had happened to the young woman who'd had such a powerful effect on such a strong, confident man as Daniel. She was truly surprised, though, when she heard herself ask, "What happened?" Once the question was out, she averted her head. This level of communication always made her feel ill at ease.

Daniel, however, caught her chin and made her look at him. "Don't regret asking that. I want to tell you, because I think it'll help you get to know me better. And I want that very much. Almost as much as I want to learn about you."

He took a quick sip of water and continued in a low voice, "Angelina was pregnant. She didn't tell me because she knew I'd insist on getting married immediately, regardless of what my family said. I guess you could say she didn't think she was good enough for me, either." He closed his dark eyes briefly, and when they opened there was a memory of pain in them. "She couldn't afford a good abortionist—so I lost both of them, Angelina and the baby. And, ultimately, my family, too, for sixteen long years."

Daniel experienced an odd sense of release as he finished speaking. It was as though some lingering vestiges of the hurt and guilt and anger had finally been lifted from his soul. And he suspected the reason lay with the woman who was looking at him now with such utter compassion in her eyes. All her reserve seemed to have vanished, for the moment at least, and he knew an aching happiness mixed with a sweet surge of pure desire. Lord, how he wanted her.

Kerith sensed that leap of passion in Daniel as surely as she felt the nascent stirrings in her own body. And she knew he would kiss her if she didn't say something. What surprised her was her reluctance to break the spell of intimacy that held them in thrall. "Ali told me you've never married," she said at last. "Was Angelina the reason?"

A shadow flickered in Daniel's clear, dark eyes before he answered. "Partly, yes. After the initial shock of her death wore off, I discovered I was just as angry with Angelina for deceiving me as I was with my father for his obstinacy. Since then, I've known a lot of women, but none of them ever meant anything to me." He hesitated, his mouth a little grim. "And I made sure none of them got pregnant by me."

An awkward silence stretched between them, and he tried to break it with a rueful chuckle. "What a hell of a thing to tell you, just when I've been working so hard to win your trust, right? My only justification is that I want you to know you're different, Kerith. That's why no other woman will do. That's why I'm not giving up on you."

Kerith felt a little frisson of anxiety at the determination she read in his smile, but before she could say anything to disavow his claim, a sharp rap sounded on her office door. "I'd better see who that is. Charlotte must be out to lunch, otherwise she'd have buzzed me on the intercom."

Arthur Kingston waited for her on the other side of the door, his expression grave. "I'm sorry to interrupt."

Kerith thought she detected a brief flash of anger in his eyes when he looked past her to where Daniel sat casually on the floor, but Arthur's next words made her forget that worry.

"There's been an accident involving one of the limos, and our driver's been hurt. I thought you'd want to know right away." He handed her a message slip from the dispatcher.

Concern for her injured employee immediately took precedence over her other worries. "You were right. I'm glad you didn't wait to tell me." By the time she thanked Arthur and got the door closed again, Daniel had begun gathering up the remains of their lunch.

"I'm really sorry, but I've got to go see about this," she said, waving the message like a truce flag.

"I understand. I own a business, too, remember?" Daniel finished repacking the basket, scooped up his jacket and tie and joined her by the door. "You can, however, make it up to me by coming over to my garage tonight."

"Your garage? Whatever for?"

"Avanti's garage," he corrected with a wink. "I started working on the Rolls . . . I mean, the Duchess, myself last night, and I'd like to show you where I think the problem might be."

Given the tone of their last conversation, Kerith was instantly wary at the prospect of being alone with Daniel Avanti in a deserted building, especially at night. "I don't know . . ." she hedged.

"Did the story of my lurid past disgust you so much that you're afraid to be alone with me?"

She glanced at him, ready to laugh, then didn't when she saw he was serious. His unexpected vulnerability prompted her to offer a swift, forceful denial. "Of course not."

Daniel's smile brightened the room by several thousand candlepower. "Then come tonight and give me a chance to show you how talented I am—as a mechanic."

Some of Kerith's wariness returned. "No ulterior motives? I haven't changed my mind about not becoming involved with you."

"No ulterior motives. Unless you consider it a motive that I enjoy your company." He grinned and tapped her on the nose. "See you around eight. And wear something you don't mind getting dirty. I may put you to work."

For the rest of the day, as she waded through insurance forms and police reports from the accident, Kerith waffled over whether or not she should have accepted Daniel's invitation. In the end, she decided it would be safe enough to go. After all, as invitations went, it wasn't exactly full of sensual promise. He had said he was working on the Rolls. How erotic could a dirty old garage be?

4

AVANTI'S GARAGE was immaculate. Kerith noticed that the minute she stepped inside the vast, dimly lit building. She also felt as if she were entering one of the few remaining bastions of machismo. Women's liberation and female mechanics aside, the place was unquestionably masculine. The smell of gasoline, oil and rich leather upholstery lent an accent of male power to the air that made her feel at a distinct disadvantage.

"You must be Kerith." The young mechanic who'd admitted her to the locked building offered a friendly grin. "I was just leaving, but Daniel's still here. He's down in the last stall, where the bright light is." Obviously anxious to be on his way, the young man stepped outside, then turned and gave a casual wave. "Nice meeting you." Before Kerith could respond, he was gone, relocking the door behind him. Moments later she heard a truck start up and drive off.

As the sound died away Kerith realized she and Daniel were probably the only two people left in the huge building, and her strongest impulse was to follow his mechanic out the door. But even as the thought occurred, she discarded it. The door had a dead bolt secured with a key from outside. She could get out, but she had no way of relocking the door. And a quick glance down the long center aisle told her a locked door was a necessity.

Lining either side of the aisle were work stalls containing some of the most exotic and expensive automobiles ever invented. Just like a stable, she thought, except the kind of horsepower housed here was fueled by gasoline. Avanti's Foreign Auto Service probably brought in a fortune in routine maintenance fees alone. Knowledge of Daniel's financial power only added to her unease at meeting him on his own turf. In the safety of her office, she'd convinced herself she could control the situation, now she wasn't so sure.

As she made her way toward the bright light at the end of the building, however, she was oddly reassured by the sound of a soft-jazz radio station and a low, melodic whistling—obviously Daniel's. And then she saw the Duchess in the stall right next to the one the mechanic had indicated, and her anxiety eased a little more. The Rolls was elevated on a hoist, and Kerith was struck by how naked and vulnerable the venerable old car looked with its underbelly exposed. *Poor Duchess. I know just how you feel.*

She nearly jumped out of her skin a second later when the sound of metal striking metal rang out, followed by a pithy expletive. Cautiously, she stepped around the wall of the last stall and discovered a dashing, vintage sports car, its front wheels on a ramp to allow space for the male body lying beneath it.

Well, half a male body, Kerith corrected herself. Two long, well-muscled legs and a definitely male pelvis incased in blue coveralls were in full view. As she watched in utter fascination, one leg flexed at the knee, drawing fabric taut over the unmistakably masculine bulge at the junction of those magnificent thighs. Daniel's thighs. She recognized them as easily as she'd recognized his voice a moment earlier when he'd cursed. But it was the part of himself he was unknowingly calling attention to that held her eye.

Normally, she didn't look at men down there. Not that she was a prude. She'd seen nude men in art and movies, and had even looked at a few on the beach in France the summer she'd vacationed there. But looking at the evidence of Daniel's masculinity, even when it was appropriately shielded by cloth, caused a primal surge of heat in her blood.

"Oh, help!"

Kerith didn't realize she'd actually voiced the thought until she heard a startled, "Wha...," followed by a dull thud and a pained, "Ouch, dammit." Before she could think to move, Daniel slid out from under the car, his big torso riding easily on a mechanic's creeper. With one slightly grimy hand he rubbed his temple, with the other pushed himself to a sitting position.

"Kerith!" His pained expression shifted quickly to a welcoming smile. "Sorry, but I didn't hear you come in. Guess I had the radio too loud." He frowned slightly. "By the way, how did you get in? The door was supposed to be locked."

"It was... is," Kerith said lamely, wondering if he could see the flush on her cheeks. "One of your employees was leaving as I arrived, and he let me in. I... I'm sorry if I made you bump your head." Kerith took a step backward. Coming here had been complete foolishness on her part. Now she had to find a graceful way to get out—fast!

"I see you came prepared to work." Daniel's dark eyes held a hint of amusement as he perused her age-softened jeans and faded "I love Las Vegas" T-shirt. He got up with enviable ease and nodded toward the adjoining stall. "Come on, I'll show you what I'm doing with the Rolls."

As he moved toward her, Kerith's apprehension grew. Hastily, she backed away on the pretense of allowing him room to pass. "I don't want to interfere with your work on someone else's car," she said, glancing at the sports car he'd been lying under. "We can do this another time."

"No problem, that one's mine. I bought it and restored it when I was living on the east coast." He favored the car with an affectionate glance. "It's a 1952 Jaguar XK 120. Like it?"

In that, at least, Kerith didn't see any need to hide her true feelings. "I love it. I think I saw one like it at the Imperial Palace's auto museum." Using the car as an excuse to put more space between them, Kerith walked over and lightly stroked the gleaming white finish of one long, down-sloping fender. "Gus introduced me to the museum years ago, and I've been a fan of vintage cars ever since."

"Then that's two things we have in common," Daniel said, as he continued toward the Rolls. The car had been elevated to accommodate his height, and when he reached a point under the front end, he turned and beckoned to her with one finger. "Come over here, and you can learn something about your own antique."

Kerith started toward him warily. "If you think my interest in cars includes any ability to fix them, I'm afraid you're mistaken. Which means we have only one thing in common."

Daniel arched one black eyebrow, and let his gaze rest on her mouth for a telling minute. Immediately her lips were suffused with a tingling warmth. "Mechanical skill wasn't the other thing I had in mind," he said in a velvety drawl. "But that isn't why I asked you here. My purpose tonight is to convince you I'm doing everything I can to make sure the Duchess gets fixed and stays fixed this time." He grinned down at her as she joined him. "Of course, I'm also glad for the chance to see you."

Kerith decided it would be wisest to ignore his last remark. Looking pointedly up at the Rolls, she said, "Tell me what's wrong with my car."

Daniel promptly adopted a more businesslike tone. "I think your problem is a short somewhere in the electrical harness. That sort of failure is often intermittent and can be a real pain to trace. Which explains why my service manager kept sending the car back to you, claiming it was fixed."

He paused, and pointed to a cylindrical piece of machinery bolted to the side of the engine. "The starter motor is the most logical place to begin looking. Unfortunately, I won't be able to start on it until tomorrow. I can't get the motor out without help, and the guy who was supposed to assist me just left on a minor family emergency."

"You mean, you intend to work on the Rolls yourself?" Kerith eyed him incredulously. "I thought the boss was supposed to sit around and give orders."

"Normally, I do." Daniel's voice lowered seductively, and the smile he gave her made Kerith's knees feel weak. "But this is a special case, for a special lady."

"That isn't fair," she said, quickly turning her face away. "You're trying to make me feel obligated to you."

"Oh, for heaven's sake." Daniel gestured impatiently.

"Well, aren't you?" Kerith insisted, rounding on him. "How do you expect me to feel, knowing you're devoting your free time to fixing my car?"

Daniel made a frustrated sound. "I don't know— friendly, maybe? Look, if it'll make you feel better, you can help me."

"I don't know the first thing about fixing cars."

"You don't have to. I'll tell you exactly what to do."

Kerith started to protest further, but Daniel was already grasping her hands and tugging them upward. "All you have to do is put your hands up here and hold the starter in place while I remove the bolts. Once they're free, I'll be able to grab the thing and get it out myself. It's heavy, but as long as you hold it still, the drive pinion that connects it to the engine will take most of the weight. Whatever you do, though, don't let go once I get the first bolt out. I don't relish the idea of having the thing fall on my head. One bump a night is enough." His large hands felt strong and capable as they pressed against the backs of her smaller ones, positioning them on either side of the starter.

"Wait a minute," Kerith hedged. "Are you sure this is safe?"

"Relax. You don't have a thing to worry about." He paused to give her a wicked grin. "Unless you're allergic to getting your hands a little dirty. This isn't exactly the cleanest part of the car."

Kerith wasn't quite sure why she didn't lower her hands and walk away from him right then. Maybe it was the light challenge in his last words. Or maybe it was her stronger need to avoid being in his debt. Whatever the reason, she gave him an arch smile and said, "If you can take it, I can."

She rued those words a moment later, when Daniel pulled a wrench from his pocket and reached up to unfasten the first bolt. The action brought their bodies into breathtaking proximity. So close, Kerith could feel his warmth, even through the layers of their clothing. Standing there, with her abdomen separated from his by less than an inch, her arms trapped in an upraised position, she had never felt more sexually vulnerable in her life. Worse yet, the idea excited rather than repelled her. Biting her lower lip in chagrin, she tried to concentrate on watching Daniel's deft movements as he loosened the bolts overhead. But all was lost when his exertions, finally, inevitably caused his broad chest to brush against her breasts. At first contact, her nipples contracted with a stinging intensity that forced a soft gasp from her lips.

The sound caught Daniel's attention just as the last bolt came free, and he looked down at her inquiringly as the weight of the starter settled against her palms.

Unable to move, she watched his eyes slowly darken in recognition of their enforced intimacy.

"Kerith . . ." Daniel's voice was a deep, sensual rumble. She saw his head begin to lower toward her and had time for one breathless, "No!" before his mouth caught hers with a fierce need.

For Kerith, the first instant of contact was volatile, causing an explosion of the pent-up feelings she had struggled with for days. Liquid fire invaded her bloodstream as Daniel's mouth ground against hers with a desperation that compelled her to open eagerly and accept the plunging invasion of his tongue. She felt his arms wrap around her, bringing their bodies into even closer contact. Her breasts were crushed against the unyielding strength of Daniel's chest, a wonderfully satisfying pressure that caused a wild quivering deep in the pit of her stomach.

This was what had been keeping her restless and wakeful at night for the past week, she thought vaguely. This hunger, this irresistible need. How could anyone fight it? Why would they even try? Insulated by a hot haze of sensation, Kerith wasn't inclined to analyze further, but a sudden sharp pain in her shoulders accomplished what years of caution could not. Uttering a low cry that ended up in Daniel's mouth, she was suddenly aware of the burden her arms still supported overhead.

"Daniel, please," she gasped when he released her mouth for a moment. "My arms...I can't hold this thing up much longer. My hands are getting numb."

It took only an instant for Daniel to comprehend and respond. "Oh, hell!" His arms shot up to take the weight of the starter motor, which had started to slip. "I'm sorry, love. Kissing you must do something to my memory. For a minute there I completely forgot this thing." He grinned apologetically and lowered the bulky piece of machinery to the ground.

So did I, Kerith thought with a rising sense of self-disgust. Numbly she noted the labored cadence of their breathing as she cleaned her hands with the rag Daniel tossed to her. How had it happened so fast? It seemed as if one minute she'd been standing there watching the man work on her car and the next she was leaning into his kiss, resenting the barriers of clothing separating their bodies. Wanting . . .

Kerith shuddered and chanced a look at Daniel, who was scrubbing at his hands with a second rag. He looked as aroused as she felt. Damn him. He'd probably counted on this happening. The entire business with the Duchess had probably been a ploy to get her alone.

"You planned this didn't you?" she accused in a tight voice. "You manipulated me into coming here just so you could...could..."She drew a quick angry breath. "I warned you, I don't tolerate manipulators. Goodbye, Mr. Avanti." She turned and stalked toward the door, refusing to give in to an undignified urge to run.

Daniel felt as if he'd been poleaxed. "Kerith, wait . . . dammit!" He nearly tripped over the starter in his haste to follow her. What had happened to his self-control? he wondered irritably as he broke into a jog. He'd promised himself—hell, he'd promised Kerith— he wouldn't rush things. But when he'd heard that sexy little gasp and looked down to see the glow of awareness in her eyes, it was as if a dam had burst inside him. His arousal had been painfully swift, demanding release. Was this a belated punishment for all the years he'd been in absolute control? Was he doomed to frustration now that he'd finally found found the woman who could inspire not only passion, but compassion in him? His temper flared. *No!*

"No!" he repeated aloud, as he caught up with Kerith, encircling her waist with both arms and swinging her off the ground. "You're not going to run away. Not until we get a few things straight."

"I was not running," Kerith retorted fiercely. The undersides of her breasts pressed softly on his arm, and her bottom bumped tantalizingly against his lingering arousal as she struggled against his hold. "But I'm not going to stay here and let you try to seduce me." Her heel connected sharply with Daniel's shin and the pain brought a flash of Italian temper.

"If I'd merely wanted to seduce you, sweetheart, I would have succeeded by now," he snapped, trapping one of her flailing legs between his hard thighs. He needn't have bothered, because in the next moment Kerith went still in his arms, her body rigid.

"Like all those other women you said you knew, but never cared about?" she inquired with cold fury. "You said I was different, but that was a lie, wasn't it? You're just like all the others, trying to control my life, using me for your own purposes, never caring about what I want, what I need."

She drew a shuddering breath, and Daniel was shocked to realize she was trembling. His anger vanished in a flood of concern. What had started as an argument over his motives had suddenly taken on much heavier connotations. He quickly set her down and turned her to face him, his hands gripping her shoulders firmly. When she refused to look at him he gave her a little shake. "What others, Kerith? Whose sins are being laid at my door?"

"Never mind. I shouldn't have said that."

"No, you're not going to stop now. Was it the orphanage? Did they treat you badly?"

Kerith's head jerked up. "How did you—"

"Ali told me," he interrupted. "Before you put the gag order on her, which seemed rather unnecessary since she didn't have much to tell. Mainly, she warned me about the high-tech defense system you've built around yourself. Who did that to you?"

She twisted against the restraint of his hands, but he wouldn't let go. "Why should I tell you? You don't really care." She looked directly at him then, and her golden eyes were filled with raw desolation—the kind of despair borne of believing no one does care. Daniel knew intuitively he was one of the few who had seen it in Kerith Ander's eyes. It made him want to spend the rest of his life convincing her she was wrong.

"I care," he said roughly, before pulling her into his arms. "I told you that in your office, today. Every time I see you I care more. Now tell me, who tried to control you and use you?"

Kerith stiffened, resisting his embrace, but she couldn't stop the trembling that seemed to vibrate her very bones. It sapped her strength and shook the walls of her reserve. She'd fought closeness for most of her life, but suddenly the struggle seemed almost more than she could bear. Her anger and wariness were replaced by a strange fatigue. She was so weary of always being on guard. How would it feel to let go, just once, and tell it all to someone? Someone who looked at her with warmth and compassion—as Daniel did?

No, no, no! She shook her head in silent denial.

"Kerith." Daniel caught her chin in an infinitely gentle grip. "What harm could it do to tell me? I'd never tell anyone else. Trust me."

She looked up and saw the inviting reassurance in his eyes, and an unexpected urge to comply temporarily overrode caution. "It started with Edelweiss," she began. The words, so long held back, came out sounding flat and lifeless. And the rest followed in the same manner, like a slow-moving stream in the first thaw of spring. The orphanage, the checks, the hopeless dreams of a lonely child, it all flowed out once she'd started.

"How long were you in the orphanage?" Daniel asked when she paused at last.

"Until I was twelve. Then I was sent to boarding schools—some of the finest in Switzerland." She tried to repress a shudder. "I hated them. Life at the orphanage wasn't ideal, but it was the only home I'd known, and the children there were all without families, like me. At school I was an oddity."

"Didn't you have any friends?"

Kerith laughed sharply. "Oh yes, I was quite popular when they found out I was an advanced student. I discovered friends could be easily purchased for the price of a difficult assignment completed, or the answers to a test. Unfortunately, the relationships never outlasted my usefulness. At first, I let it bother me, and there was . . . trouble. I was moved from one school to the next, until I discovered life was easier if I didn't allow myself to care."

She heard Daniel swear softly, and felt his hand reach to massage the tension from her shoulders, but she couldn't relax, not with the story half told.

"When I received Edelweiss's offer of a college education—with the stipulation that it be obtained in an American college—I refused to accept it at first. I spent an entire year traveling around Europe on the birthday money from Edelweiss, which had been banked for me over the years. But then I realized I had no real ties in Switzerland. And I really wanted the college education."

"But it must have taken a lot of courage, coming to a foreign country all alone," Daniel protested quietly.

Kerith shrugged dismissingly. "I survived."

"By not letting anyone get too close. That's a high price to pay."

His gentle pronouncement caused a tremor in the foundation of Kerith's self-possession, and she felt compelled to defend herself. "Not so high a price." Using her hands she forced a little distance between them. "Closeness merely invites manipulation, as you should know. Look what your family did to you and that girl you got pregnant."

Daniel looked pained. "That wasn't really manipulation. They thought they were acting in my best interest, just as Ali did when she agreed to help me meet you. True manipulation is self-centered." He smiled ruefully. "You may find this hard to believe after that kiss, but I invited you here tonight because I thought it would be a more neutral setting for getting acquainted. I don't consider a garage the ideal site for grand seduction. However..." He touched one blunt fingertip to her chin, urging her to meet his eyes. "We can't pretend that kiss didn't happen. And I suspect if you were completely honest with yourself, you'd admit you wanted it just as much as I did."

Yes, she had, Kerith thought desperately. And it was dangerous and foolish and... She didn't get a chance to finish. In the next instant all hell seemed to break loose, beginning with a loud crash just outside the building and followed immediately by the strident ringing of an alarm bell.

"Daniel, what—" She was cut off abruptly as Daniel shoved her into the shadowy darkness of a nearby service stall.

"Stay put," he ordered tersely. "Someone—or something—just tripped the security alarm. It's probably a dog or cat, but I don't believe in taking chances. We've had a few break-in attempts in the past. Don't move until I get back."

"Where are you going?" Kerith called over the clang of the alarm. A new anxiety gripped her. What if it wasn't a dog or cat? What if some criminal was out there, and Daniel...? Impulsively, she clutched his sleeve. "You're not going to do something dumb and heroic, are you?"

Daniel smiled reassuringly and put his hand over hers for a moment. "Don't worry, I'm just going to have a look around. If it's a false alarm, I need to notify the security company before they call the police. It's nice to know you care, though." He moved off with the stealth of a jungle fighter, and Kerith was left alone in the darkness to deal with those last unsettling words.

She didn't care for him, not in the way he meant, or so she told herself as she waited for his return with a pounding heart. But when the alarm cut off a short while later and Daniel reappeared looking unharmed, the surge of happiness she experienced went far beyond simple relief.

"Did you find anything?" she demanded, her whisper sounding unnaturally loud in the eerie silence enveloping the building.

"Just a trash can knocked over, most likely by some stray looking for a snack. The can must have bumped a window frame hard enough to trigger the alarm." Since he'd returned, his expression had been preoccupied, wary, now it softened. "Are you all right? You look a little shaky." He took her hand and drew her out into the soft light bathing the main aisle.

"I'm fine." Using the back of her free hand, she brushed back the tumble of golden bangs feathered over her forehead.

Daniel watched the gesture intently. "Such lovely, silky hair," he murmured. "I've wanted to touch it since I first saw it. He lifted one hand as if to do so, glanced at it and sighed. "Guess I'd better not until I've used some soap and water. In fact . . . Turn around."

"What?"

"Turn your back to me," he elaborated, then chuckled when she complied. "Your shirt looks like one of my shop rags. That alone should prove I didn't plan our passionate little interlude. I prefer lovemaking without grease."

Once again, the air between them was charged with sensual undertones, and Kerith kept her back to him while she nervously tugged at the hem of her sweatshirt. "I don't think you planned it, but that doesn't mean I think it should have happened." She gestured helplessly with both hands. "Every time I'm around you, I say or do something I shouldn't."

"Like going wild when I kiss you?"

Kerith ducked her head. "Like pouring out all the intimate details of my past. I've never done that before. And I don't think I should have done it tonight."

Daniel came up behind her and settled his hands on her shoulders. "Hey, no regrets. I think you needed to tell me almost as much as I needed to hear it. I want to be close to you, Kerith. And I don't mean in the physical sense alone, although I think we both know that's inevitable if we spend much more time together."

With an uneasy shrug, she stepped out of his reach. "You make it all sound so simple, when I know it's not. I . . . I think I should go home now." Home, where she could work it all out, alone and safe.

Daniel didn't argue further. He simply took her arm and said, "All right, I'll walk you to your car."

Nothing more was said until she had opened the door of her silver Mazda RX-7, then Daniel motioned for her to wait. "This isn't goodbye, you know. I'm going to give you a little time to think, but that doesn't mean I'm giving up. I want you, Kerith Anders." He tipped her chin up until she could see the need darkening his eyes. "Remember this while you're doing all that thinking." His kiss was a dazzling, sweet demand, and disappointingly brief. When it was over, Kerith stared at him in bemusement for a long moment, inhaled sharply, and ducked into the safety of her car. When she pulled into her own driveway a while later, she could still feel the hot imprint of his mouth on her lips.

Over the next week, she was haunted by the memory of that kiss—and every other distracting detail of her encounters with Daniel Avanti. Again and again she ordered herself to stop thinking about him, but even though he kept his word about giving her time to think, she couldn't banish him from her mind.

And the dreams she had at night! Sizzling, Technicolor fantasies that left her lying wide-eyed and breathless in the damp tangle of her flower-sprigged bed sheets. She felt as if she were suffering through puberty again, except now she was mature enough to know, at least in theory, what her body craved.

"The man hasn't even called me this week, and all I do is think about him," Kerith muttered irritably as she stared out her office window. The cloud-darkened Nevada sky matched her mood exactly. Of course, there had been the T-shirt, a soft lavender one with "I love Las Vegas" imprinted across the front in iridescent rainbow colors. It had arrived by special messenger with a note from Daniel that said:

This is to replace the one I ruined. Try it on and guess which letters I'd like to trace with my fingertips.

Yours hopefully,
Daniel

Just remembering it brought a hot flush to her cheeks and a frown of consternation to her brow.

"Oops! Something tells me you aren't as happy as I am to see Friday night." Ali stood poised in the doorway to Kerith's office, a tentative smile on her face.

Kerith sighed and waved her in. "I'm fine, but you may not feel quite so happy when you see the weather report. The forecast mentioned a possibility of thundershowers."

"A great night for a fireplace and free-delivery pizza. Want to join Cami and me?"

"No, thanks. After the week I've had I wouldn't be very good company. Besides, I have some paperwork to finish before I go."

Ali grimaced sympathetically. "It has been hectic, hasn't it? Especially with Arthur out the whole time."

Kerith smiled wryly. "Wasn't that ironic? You faked a sprained ankle and Arthur, who is the most coordinated man I know, actually manages to do it. Although I didn't quite believe his story about tripping over a cat. More likely he did it climbing out of some rich matron's window in the middle of the night, when her husband came home unexpectedly."

Ali gave a throaty chuckle and waved one hand. "Speaking of home, it's late and I'm going to head for mine. See you Monday."

Alone again, Kerith sat down at her desk. There was still at least an hour's work ahead of her. As if in protest, her stomach rumbled softly, reminding her she hadn't eaten since that morning's coffee and raisin toast. What she needed was a snack to hold her until she got home. Automatically, her thoughts went to the box of candy sitting in one drawer of the desk. Daniel's candy.

She'd been nibbling on it unrepentantly all week— one didn't waste gourmet chocolates, regardless of the source—and now it beckoned.

The rich chocolate coating began to melt against her fingertips as she lifted the piece of candy from the box. Raising it to her lips, she licked it delicately before sinking her teeth into the rounded center. The sharp piquance of cherry liqueur squirted into her mouth, followed immediately by the sweetness of the cherry center and the silky richness of dark chocolate. Kerith moaned helplessly, her eyes closing in near ecstasy as she slowly chewed.

"Lord, what I wouldn't give to be the one who put that look on your face."

The huskily voiced sentiment came unexpectedly, nearly causing Kerith to choke. Her eyes flew open and fastened on Daniel, who was moving toward her purposefully. "Mind if I try some?" He seated himself on the near corner of her desk and leaned toward her with his most charming smile.

Kerith swallowed quickly, tried to speak, and discovered she couldn't. Something had gone awry with her brain's circuitry from the instant she'd registered Daniel's presence, and the only message coming through at the moment was an overwhelming joy in seeing him again. So she merely nodded her assent and offered the box of candy.

Daniel had other ideas. Without warning, his head came down and his mouth captured hers, leaving her time for just one startled "Oh!" before his tongue gently pushed past her lips. He swept through her mouth like a greedy marauder, gathering up the lingering sweetness of the candy, rubbing his tongue sensuously over and under hers, stroking the slick softness of her inner cheek, and testing the sharp even edge of her teeth. When he'd finished, Kerith felt as if her mouth had been ravished.

Gasping, she collapsed against the soft backrest of her chair and searched for something to say. Daniel beat her to it.

"I don't think I've ever tasted anything sweeter. Come on, let's get out of here." He tugged Kerith out of her chair, scooped up her purse, and was halfway to the door before she dug in her heels and stopped.

"Not so fast, Mr. Avanti. Just where do you think you're dragging me?"

Daniel looked down at the stubborn set of her chin and grinned. "I wondered how long it would take you to come out of that daze. We're going for a ride, if you must know. I think I managed to find the electrical problem in your Rolls, and I need to test-drive it. I thought the least you could do is come with me, since it is your car."

Kerith's eyes narrowed consideringly. "A test run. Are you sure that's all it will be?"

"No." Daniel's expression sobered. "It's been a damned long week, Kerith. I'm starved for your company." One dark brow arched suggestively. "And judging by that kiss, just now, I think you're a little hungry, too." He carefully placed the purse in her hand and released her.

"You've had a whole week to think things over and I suspect your decision was made before I walked in here tonight. I won't, however, be accused of forcing you to do anything against your will." He walked to the door, then looked back at her, his hand held out invitingly. "Are you coming?"

A small lifetime seemed to pass before Kerith in the moments she stood there looking at Daniel's outstretched hand. A speeded-up review of the events and decisions that had made her what she was, and what she was not. As she weighed the evidence, she couldn't escape a feeling of deficiency—that she'd been cheated of something essential.

Before Daniel had arrived in her life, she'd found peace and security in her isolation. But with a few kisses, he'd given her a taste of the things she'd lost in her quest for safety. He was offering a chance to make up for that loss. Did she dare take it?

"I'm coming," she announced firmly, crossing the room to place her hand in Daniel's warm grasp. But as she followed him outside, she couldn't escape the feeling that she was stepping into an alien territory, from which there might be no return.

5

"JUST HOW LONG does a test run take?" Kerith asked, twisting to face Daniel from the passenger side of the Rolls's richly upholstered front seat. He had taken the wheel, with her permission, and for the past ten minutes the Duchess had been humming along under his competent hand. Now they were on Boulder Highway, which led out of the city in a southeasterly direction, and Kerith had begun to wonder when he would turn back.

At her question, Daniel gave her a guileless smile and said, "There isn't a set time or distance. I thought we'd run out to Hoover Dam."

"Hoover Dam!" Kerith couldn't hide her dismay. She'd committed herself to spending some time with Daniel, but this was more than she'd expected. "That's a forty-minute drive. And look at those storm clouds. We could get some really nasty weather tonight."

Daniel dismissed her objections with a careless wave of his hand. "You've lived in the desert too long. Every time anyone around here sees an overcast sky he thinks it's time to start building an ark. I'll bet you didn't react like this when you were in Switzerland."

"I don't want to talk about Switzerland. I did more than enough of that a week ago." Even now, the memory made her uncomfortable. Shifting uneasily in her seat, she turned her attention to the night-shaded view outside her window. The flat valley floor was gradually giving way to barren foothills, and beyond them she saw the sharp silhouette of the mountain range sheltering Lake Mead.

"Kerith, please don't withdraw from me now. I don't think I could stand it." Daniel's softly voiced plea brought her eyes back to his strong profile.

He was serious, she realized in surprise. And vulnerable, maybe as vulnerable as she was to him. "I'm not withdrawing, exactly," she responded quietly. "But I can't rush into . . . this. I'm not used to sharing my life with anyone."

Daniel reached out and gently squeezed her tightly clenched hands as they lay in her lap. "I understand. Unfortunately, that means you're stuck with hearing more of the boring details of my life."

Kerith laughed and pulled her hands from beneath his, ostensibly to stifle a fake yawn. But her real goal was to hide the shivering excitement his touch had caused. An excitement that seemed to grow even after the contact was ended.

Daniel didn't appear to notice. After returning his hand to the steering wheel, he proceeded to entertain her with some of the current exploits of his extended family. From there he went into a droll recounting of Avanti history.

As they climbed higher and higher on a road that twisted through rock-scarred slopes, Kerith was drawn deeper and deeper into the web of Daniel's charming narrative. By the time they'd reached the curving downward stretch of road leading to the dam, she'd nearly forgotten her reservations about being alone with him.

And they were alone, she noted, as Daniel drove the limousine past a succession of deserted parking lots, and a snack and a souvenir stand with a Closed sign in the window. When he reached the lot nearest the dam, he parked and turned toward her with a self-conscious grin. "Are you sorry for getting me started on my family? You've been kind of quiet, and you don't look very entertained."

Outside, the only sign of life was a few pieces of trash dancing across the pavement under the force of a gusting wind. But the interior of the car was alive with the familiarity that had been steadily growing between them. Knowing where that familiarity could lead, Kerith decided it would be safest to keep him talking about his family. "I wasn't bored," she said, with a small shake of her head. "I was just thinking about how much you seem to care for your family, and how difficult it must have been for you being separated from them all the years you were gone."

In the dim light from the parking lot's overhead fixtures, Kerith saw a flicker of pain tighten his features.

"Those were the emptiest years of my life," Daniel admitted in a low voice.

"Couldn't you have patched things up with your father, somehow?"

"Maybe." Daniel hesitated. How much could he tell her? Would she turn away in disgust if she knew of his life as Casanova? Most likely. And yet, he was suddenly seized by a compulsion to confess, to lay himself bare before her and hope for understanding. After the way she'd opened up to him the other night, it seemed only fair.

"That wasn't the only reason I stayed away," he went on carefully. "Before I wised up and stopped trying to make others pay for the mistakes Angelina and my father made, I got myself involved in a situation that nearly destroyed my self-image. For a long time I wasn't able to face myself, let alone my family."

A heavy, expectant silence settled over the interior of the car. Just like a confessional, Daniel thought ruefully. Then he heard Kerith draw a slow breath, and her question—when it came—held an unexpected note of sympathy. "What did you do?"

And when he looked into her lovely golden eyes and saw the genuine empathy there, he knew he was going to tell her, regardless of the fact that it probably was the riskiest step he'd ever taken. He couldn't tell her everything, of course, but he had to give her something to equal the confidences she'd offered a week ago, and the gift of caring she was offering now. It was the least he could do, in light of the deception he must continue until Edelweiss made an appearance.

He sighed and rubbed a hand over his face. "My job with the government wasn't as straightforward as I originally led you to believe. I did a lot of top-level security work."

"You were a spy?"

Daniel winced. "The accepted term is agent, but yes, I did some spying."

"Did it involve killing? Is that why you couldn't face your family?" Uncertainty vibrated in her soft query, and the sound cut deep into Daniel's soul. What he had done was bad enough, but to have her think him a killer was too much.

"I never killed anyone. At least not after I left the Marines," he denied quickly. "Sometimes, though, I felt as if I'd condemned a few." *Stop now,* an inner voice warned. *Only a fool would tell her the rest.*

Kerith looked confused. "Condemned? How?"

Daniel opened his mouth to speak and realized his heart was pounding at a rate normally reserved for moments of imminent physical danger. His palms were sweaty, too, and he rubbed them dry on his slacks before gripping the wheel of the car. "What would you say if I told you my code name was Casanova? And that I earned it seducing secrets out of unsuspecting women?"

A stunned silence followed, and he knew with a dreadful certainty that he'd gone too far. Blown it. No woman would welcome that kind of news about a man she was seeing, let alone a woman who had strong reservations about a relationship in the first place. How could he have believed otherwise? He'd be lucky if she let him have a ride back to town, at this point. On top of that, how was he going to tell Lucretia he'd blown his contact?

"What kind of women?" Kerith's low-pitched question barely penetrated the thick miasma of his self-disgust.

Daniel sighed heavily. "All kinds. Lady scientists who worked for unfriendly nations, idealistic young women who thought they could change our government by passing top-secret information to our enemies. You name it, I probably encountered it."

"Did . . . did you make love to all of them?"

"Not all." Daniel considered leaving it at that, then figured, what the hell he might as well tell the whole sordid story. "In the beginning, when I didn't care, there were quite a few. But toward the end, when I realized what I'd become... well, it just didn't happen. I became quite adept at getting the information I wanted before things progressed to the bedroom." He laughed harshly. "The funniest part was, as the bedding frequency went down, my reputation as a tireless lover grew." He chanced a look at Kerith, and found her regarding him thoughtfully.

"Does your family know about this?"

"No. They all believe I had a nice respectable job. You're the only person I've told." What was that look in her eyes? Disgust? Dismay?

"Why are you telling me?"

Daniel took a slow cautious breath. "Because I thought you had a right to know. I care very deeply for you, and I wanted honesty between us before we make love." *Please forgive me, love, that it can't be complete honesty,* he added silently.

"If you can't accept what I was, I'll understand," he continued out loud. "But I want you to know I've changed. And I'm trying to make up for the mistakes I made."

Kerith saw the anxiety tightening Daniel's expression as he waited for her response, and she felt a flutter of panic. She hadn't expected this kind of intimacy when she'd accepted his invitation. It disturbed her more than his confident assumption that they would make love. And yet, his confession seemed strangely appropriate, after her soul-baring of a week ago. She cleared her throat nervously. "I'm not sure I know what you want me to say."

"Just tell me whether or not my past is going to be a problem for you."

Kerith considered that, and finally shook her head. "My life hasn't been perfect. I wouldn't presume to judge yours. In fact, I think you're being a little too hard on yourself. What you did—it was supposedly done to help your government, wasn't it?"

Daniel snorted softly. "In my more forgiving moments I allow myself to believe that. Your vote of confidence means a lot, though." He smiled suddenly and grabbed her hand. "In fact, I feel better than I have in a long time. Come on, let's go look at the dam."

Kerith gasped in protest, as he flung open the car door and got out, tugging her out behind him on the driver's side. "It's cold and windy out here, and we're not exactly dressed for sight-seeing."

As if to prove her point, a fierce gust of wind buffeted them, whipping at the hem of her pink linen coatdress, and raising the tails of Daniel's beige sport coat. Daniel didn't appear to notice. He simply laughed and wrapped an arm around her as they proceeded down to the walkway crossing the dam. Once there, he astounded her by bracing himself against the railing and bursting into a lusty Irish sea chantey.

When she laughingly questioned his sanity, he grinned and replied, "I always feel as if I'm on the bow of a great ship when I come up here. Makes me want to sing."

When Kerith looked out over the dark, choppy water, she had to admit it did feel like standing at the rail of a huge luxury liner. She started to tell him so, but all of a sudden the heavy clouds above them unloaded a deluge of rain, and they had to make a mad dash for the Rolls.

"It was your singing," she teased, as they scrambled into the front seat, dripping wet and laughing helplessly.

Daniel pretended to glare at her, while using both hands to comb back his wet hair. "I'll have you know some people think I have a very good singing voice."

And he did, Kerith thought, squeezing water from her own drenched hair. His singing perfectly matched the rich baritone of his speaking voice. "All right, Caruso," she conceded with a grin. "You can serenade me all the way home. Just get this car started so we can turn the heater on."

Giving her a cocky little salute, Daniel moved to comply. But when he turned the key in the ignition, he was rewarded with an ominous click. When he'd gotten the same result on the second, third and fourth tries, he leaned his head back against the seat and groaned. "To think I actually wished for this sort of thing to happen when I was in high school." He gave Kerith a worried look. "You don't think I planned this, do you?"

Kerith eyed their bedraggled clothing and laughed. "No. I would, however, like to know what you plan to do next."

"Look under the hood, I guess," Daniel said, sighing in resignation. "Do you happen to have a flashlight?" When Kerith produced one from under the seat, he grinned and added, "How about a raincoat and umbrella?"

"There should be a slicker in the trunk. Anything I can do to help?"

"No, stay here. There's no point in both of us being out in that."

But when he'd been tinkering under the hood for ten minutes, with no result, Kerith got out and joined him. "You can't accomplish anything, with it raining like this," she shouted over the roaring wind. "There's a public phone outside that snack stand we passed on the way down. I'll go call for help."

Swearing softly, Daniel gave in and slammed down the hood. "You get back in the car. I'll make the call. After all, it was my idea to come up here." He got her settled in the backseat, with a blanket he found in the trunk, then started up the hill at a slow, splashing jog.

A long twenty minutes later he was back, streaming water like Niagara Falls and trying not to shiver as he joined her in the backseat and closed the door. "Who would have believed the weather could get so bad so fast," he grumbled, accepting the small towel Kerith had borrowed from the mini-bar.

"Not I," she assured him, her eyes twinkling. "Did you find the phone?"

"Yes, and it actually worked." Daniel's reply came out muffled as he scrubbed his face and hair with the inadequate piece of terry. "My brother-in-law will be here as soon as possible. In this filthy weather, that could be an hour or more, so I guess we're stuck for the moment." He sneezed, and a shiver ran down his large frame as he shrugged out of the dripping slicker and his sport coat. Fortunately, his shirt and slacks appeared to be merely damp.

"You must be nearly frozen," Kerith said, instantly concerned. "Here, take the blanket. I'll be fine without it."

"Absolutely not. It's my fault we're in this mess. If you got sick, I'd never forgive myself."

"Don't be ridiculous. I chose to come." She pulled the blanket from around her shoulders and pushed it toward him. "Now take it."

"All right." Daniel accepted the blanket reluctantly. Then, before she knew what he intended, he grasped her waist with both hands and hauled her unceremoniously onto his lap. "But only if we share."

"Daniel!" Kerith's squawk of protest was cut off when the blanket settled over her head, cocooning her against his broad chest. His laughter rumbled beneath her ear, and when she tried to push away, his strong arms formed a warm prison.

"Quit fighting me, love," he said, still chuckling. "This is the only positive aspect of the entire situation."

"Positive for you, maybe," Kerith fumed. "I can't breathe under here." The truth was, she could breathe; the result was the problem. With each inhalation her nose was filled with pure essence of Daniel, and it was having an incendiary effect on her system.

"Sweetheart, if you don't stop squirming your sweet bottom around on my lap, I'm going to get a lot warmer than I intended."

Kerith's head came up so hard, she managed to break free of the blanket's smothering confines, but that only served to put her in most intimate proximity with

Daniel's smiling mouth. "Do you know what I'd like right now?" he murmured.

"No, what?" Kerith's heart went into overdrive, and her mind did an instant replay of the kiss they'd shared in her office.

"Champagne," he replied, leaning over her to pull a bottle out of the Rolls's tiny refrigerator. Somehow, he managed to unwrap and pull the cork without loosening his hold on her.

"Very professional, sir. But I hardly think it's appropriate for our circumstances."

"*Au contraire, mademoiselle.* Champagne always tastes better in the middle of a storm at Hoover Dam." After some rummaging, he located a stemmed glass and filled it with the effervescent liquid. "Especially when I'm with a beautiful woman. Here, drink."

Given the choice of either drinking or having the chilly stuff dumped on her, Kerith wisely chose the former. The combination of icy cold liquid and tingling bubbles made her shudder at first, but only moments later the wine hit her empty stomach, resulting in an instant rush of warmth. Apparently satisfied with the drink she'd taken, Daniel lowered the glass and drank himself, resting his lips on the exact spot hers had touched.

"Mmm, champagne and Kerith Anders, two of my favorite flavors." He refilled the glass and offered it to her again. This time she didn't balk, not even when he insisted she down at least a third of glass.

"I think you're right," Kerith said a little breathlessly, after swallowing. "This champagne tastes better than any I can remember."

"Really? Let me taste." Without further warning, Daniel's mouth came down on hers with a hunger that had nothing to do with food or drink. And just as quickly Kerith felt an answering need rise within her, compelling her to open her lips to the bold thrust of his tongue.

He tasted of rain and champagne and the essence she craved most of all—Daniel. She was dimly aware when he reached to set down the champagne flute, and then his hand returned to add to the magic his mouth was creating. Slowly, he stroked the curves and planes of her body, warming her in spite of her cold damp clothing. And when his hand settled on her breast, Kerith was flooded by a heat that transcended mere physical warmth.

"Damn, I keep forgetting just how potent your kisses are," Daniel gasped, when he broke away last. His mouth brushed hers again lightly, as if he couldn't quite bring himself to stop. "When you agreed to come with me tonight, I told myself I wouldn't rush things, but self-control isn't easy around a woman like you."

"A man like Casanova out of control? I find that hard to believe."

"I'm not Casanova anymore," he said gruffly, and bent to press a kiss on the soft curve of her throat. "I'm just a man who happens to go a little crazy when he's with you." His fingers flexed gently on her breast, and Kerith moaned at the pleasure surging through her body.

"So incredibly lovely," Daniel murmured against her lips, as he deftly undid the front buttons on her dress and slipped his fingers inside to trace the satiny swell of flesh that strained against the low-cut cup of her bra. He found the tight bud of her nipple beneath the lacy material, and his descending mouth caught Kerith's helpless cry of need. This time, the stroke of his tongue was more eloquent, telling her of the ultimate invasion he desired. Beneath her thigh she felt the swelling heat of his arousal, and a quivering need pulsed to life between her thighs. She shifted impatiently, wanting more, wishing . . .

A sharp rap sounded against the rear window, startling them both to sudden awareness. Daniel swore softly, and hastily pulled his hand out of her dress. "We've got company love. Perhaps you'd better sit next to me until I find out who it is." He needn't have made the suggestion. Kerith was already off his lap and huddled in the far corner of the seat, embarrassment and dismay already cooling the fire of abandon.

When Daniel rolled the foggy window down a crack, she caught a glimpse of a security guard, who kindly inquired if they were having car trouble and offered aid. He didn't linger after Daniel assured him help was on the way.

"Nice to know someone is nearby," Daniel commented, as he rolled up the window. "But the timing was lousy." His easy grin faded when he saw the look on Kerith's face. "Hey, don't let it upset you. He couldn't see a thing with the windows steamed up the way they are."

"It isn't only that." Kerith lowered her gaze to her lap. "I was thinking of what might have happened if we hadn't been interrupted just then. What would that man have found if he'd shown up ten or fifteen minutes later?" She threw him a slightly belligerent look. "I wasn't thinking of stopping, were you?"

Her unexpected honesty charmed him into a smile, and he reached over and dragged her close for a hug, before she had time to resist. "I have to admit, I lost control for a while there. But I like to believe I would have stopped short of making love to you in the back seat of a car, even if it is a Rolls-Royce." He cupped her cheek tenderly and turned her to face him. "You deserve better than that. Our first time together is going to be very special."

"You say that as if it's a certainty," Kerith mumbled, suddenly reminded of her lack of experience. "I think I'd better warn you, I haven't had much . . . practice at this. I won't be able to measure up to the other women you've known."

Daniel twisted around to cup her face with both hands. "Don't even think of comparing yourself to them. What happened before meant nothing to me. I want you, Kerith Anders. I want you more than I've wanted any other woman. So much so, that at times I even forget the basic niceties of seduction."

"Are you going to seduce me?" she inquired in a shaky voice. The thought sent a thrill to the center of her being.

"No. Casanova seduced women. I'm going to make love with you." He planted a quick kiss on her lips and released her face, then drew her tightly to his side, with one arm. "And that precludes groping in the backseat of a car. Until we can get out of here, I'll have to settle for champagne and the pleasure of your company."

To Kerith's surprise, he did just that. Outside the storm escalated to a howling gale, yet inside the car there was an atmosphere of comfort and security she wouldn't have believed possible. The passion still glowed within her, but it was banked, put into abeyance. When Daniel's brother-in-law arrived a while later, his eyes twinkling at their predicament, she found she could actually laugh at his jokes about Las Vegas weather.

They arrived at Daniel's condo in the middle of a torrential downpour, and Kerith quickly agreed to Daniel's offer to drive her home from there, allowing the tow truck to proceed directly to Avanti's garage. By the time she and Daniel reached his front step, they were both soaked to the skin.

"Whew! I'd forgotten how fierce these desert storms can be," Daniel gasped. He quickly opened the door and hustled Kerith inside.

"Given our normally dry climate, it's easy to forget." She smiled as she skinned her wet hair back from her face, but her expression turned to dismay when she saw the huge puddle she was creating on the white tiled floor. "I think you'd better take me home right away. I'm going to cause a flood in here."

"A little water never hurt anything," Daniel replied easily. He bent and tugged off his sodden shoes and socks, then started unbuttoning his shirt. "And I don't intend to go anywhere until I have a hot shower and some dry clothes." He peered at her critically. "You look as if you could use the same."

Until that moment, she hadn't been aware she was shivering. "I . . . I'll be all right," she said quickly, her wanton mind instantly filled with pictures of them showering together. Contrarily, her body chose to betray her just then, with a sneeze.

"Sure, you will," Daniel agreed, taking her arm and urging her down the hallway to a small bathroom that contained a shower. "You can use this one. I'll take the one upstairs. I have a robe you can borrow until your things dry."

Kerith perused her dripping wet dress. "Unless you have a clothes dryer, that could take a long time. And I'll just get wet again when you take me home."

"I don't have a dryer," Daniel said quietly. His dark eyes were suddenly intent as he reached to cup her cheek with one large, warm hand. "I was hoping I might be able to convince you to stay, at least until the rain eases a bit." He must have seen the apprehension that instantly tightened her body, because he added, "I'm not going to ask for anything you aren't ready to give. If you like, we can just sit in front of my fireplace until it's safer to drive."

Such an uncomplicated offer, on the surface, Kerith thought. But she knew, even if Daniel didn't, that by agreeing to stay she would be taking the last step toward becoming intimate with him. It wasn't an easy step, after so many years of caution, but the touch of his hand against her cheek felt so warm, so right. And as she stared into the depths of his midnight eyes and saw the undisguised need there, desire came simmering up to the surface of her consciousness, burning away any lingering restraint.

"I think I'll accept the loan of that robe," she murmured, moving into the bathroom and closing the door behind her. "You can leave it outside the door."

When she stepped out of the bathroom twenty minutes later, she was warm and dry and bundled up in a navy velour robe that swamped her slender frame. Even her hair had been dried, courtesy of the blow dryer Daniel had thoughtfully left at the door with his robe. All in all, she felt a lot less vulnerable than she had expected as she ventured down the hall, looking for her host.

She found him in the living room, which opened off the hall to the right. He was sprawled comfortably on the couch, staring into the bright flames that filled the white brick fireplace. It offered the only light in the darkened room. His loafer-clad feet were propped casually on a glass-topped coffee table, and next to them stood two mugs filled with steaming liquid.

Some sixth sense must have warned him of her silent, barefoot approach, because he turned with a glowing smile and beckoned her to join him. "You're just in time. The cappuccino was getting cold."

Kerith settled herself cautiously on the cushion next to his and gratefully accepted the tall slender mug he offered. "I love cappuccino. How did you know?"

"I didn't. I guess it's just another of the many things we have in common."

"Maybe not so many," Kerith argued, glancing around. "This room, for instance. It's nothing like my living room." She didn't add that she hadn't decorated her living room. It had been professionally done before she married Gus, and she'd never felt the need to change it. Now, as she studied Daniel's decor, she decided she liked it better than the formal, brocaded furnishings in her place. The walls were pristine white, as was the tiled floor, but bright splashes of turquoise and gold had been added with mini-blinds and area rugs, and on the walls there were several vivid desert scenes painted by a Southwestern artist she admired.

"You don't like it." Daniel sounded a little hurt.

"Actually, I think it's fantastic." *And so are you*, she added silently as she surreptitiously studied him over the rim of her cup. He looked magnificent in the worn jeans and soft yellow sweater he'd donned after his shower. His hair, still slightly damp, had been combed carelessly back from his broad forehead and gleamed silky black in the firelight.

Physical attraction, she told herself, that's what they had in common. Of course, that didn't explain his ability to draw her into deeply personal revelations, but she didn't want to think about that now. She didn't want to think about anything but the sweet rush of returning desire that came just from looking at him—and how it would feel to have him satisfy that desire completely.

"I'm flattered you like the cappuccino, but you didn't have to drink it quite so fast." Daniel's amused comment drew her attention to the nearly empty mug she held.

Kerith blinked distractedly, the rich flavor of espresso laced with milk and amaretto just then registering on her taste buds. She smiled apologetically. "I guess I got carried away."

Daniel pulled a comically unhappy face. "And here I thought my charming presence had put that avid look in your eyes." He nodded toward her mug. "Would you like more?"

"No." Kerith's heart began to beat faster. Tell him what you want, she ordered herself silently. But the words wouldn't come.

"It's still raining pretty hard. I hope you're not going to ask me to take you home."

Before answering, Kerith carefully set her mug on the coffee table. Then, nervously clutching the thick folds of Daniel's robe, she boldly met his gaze and said, "I want to stay."

The dark brown of Daniel's eyes deepened almost to black, as comprehension dawned. A slight smile curved the corners of his mouth as he slowly reached out to draw her onto his lap. "Then why don't we see if we can find something to do to pass the time?" he murmured.

For Kerith, it felt as if she'd stepped out of an airplane at ten thousand feet. Tactile sensation swept over her like the rush of air in a mad free-fall. Daniel's fingers digging into her ribs with barely restrained force as he pulled her nearer. His mouth, warm and tender at first, then hard and hungry as his control suddenly gave way. His hands were almost rough in their urgency, as he sought her body through the thickness of the robe, then impatiently shoved the material aside, baring her breasts to the soft firelight. He touched her almost reverently at first, his voice coming in a rough growl.

"Even in my dreams I never imagined you to be this beautiful. Your skin is so lovely, like gold satin." He bent and touched the tip of his tongue to the tight bud of her nipple, and a trembling seized Kerith. And when he drew the tip of her breast into his mouth, suckling softly, then harder and harder, an ache blossomed in the pit of her belly and quickly grew unbearable.

"Oh, please," she cried, sinking her fingers into the silky depths of his hair to hold him nearer. But to her dismay, he raised his head, his breathing labored as he fought for control.

"Too fast," he managed after a moment, even as his fingers delicately tormented her throbbing nipple. "I can't believe what you do to me. One minute we're talking, and the next I can't think of anything beyond how it will feel to be deep inside you. You deserve more finesse."

"I don't want finesse," Kerith responded with a fierceness born of desperation. Her fingers tightened in his hair. Passion, so long held in check, was now in full control, demanding immediate satisfaction. And nothing—nothing—was going to stop it now. She brought her mouth to his and recklessly pushed her tongue inside, imitating the teasing movements he'd used on her. And when he groaned and took control of the kiss, she released his head and slipped her hands under his sweater, seeking the warmth of naked skin. She found it, swelled by hard muscle, roughened by masculine hair, and her touch elicited another groan from Daniel.

"Kerith, love, that feels so good . . . too good." He swung her up in his arms and stood suddenly, then placed her flat on the couch. The robe spread open around her, but she was beyond feeling modest, even when his eyes appraised her body with frank approval.

."You're tan all over. I used to dream about how you would look after I found out you swam in the nude. A golden lady...my golden lady." He knelt beside her, his hands smoothing over her skin, raising her excitement unbelievably high, until his fingers pressed into the soft, golden curls shielding her womanhood, and Kerith felt as if she'd received an electric shock. His fingertip probed delicately until he found the one tiny spot that burned for his touch. Her body arched upward convulsively, and she grabbed handfuls of Daniel's sweater, pulling until his reassuring weight was pressing down on her. Even through the material of his jeans, she could feel his arousal, hard and hot, nestled against the aching place between her thighs. Her hips flexed up, an instinctive entreaty.

"Daniel," she wailed softly. "I can't stand it. I need..."

"I know." His voice was heavy with reluctant acceptance, as his lower body lunged hard against her once. "We'll have to save the leisurely pace for another time." A moment later he was up and stripping off his clothes with hands that shook in their haste.

He stood naked before her for one eternal moment, his glorious body gilded by firelight, his phallus daunting, yet beautiful in full arousal. Then he was beside her again, naked flesh pressing warmly to hers, as his fingers sought and found the tight, moist readiness of her femininity. "Kerith, my love, relax. I don't want to hurt you."

"A-all right," she said, and then drew in a hissing breath, as his deft touch started a shivering that wouldn't stop. She squeezed her eyes shut and felt Daniel's hands urging her knees to bend and open to him. The couch cushions gave softly beneath her as he settled heavily, his manhood searching only briefly before finding its goal. And with one, long irrevocable thrust he drove home.

A startled cry escaped Kerith as her untried flesh resisted for one, painful instant—then gave way, and she was deeply, overwhelmingly filled. She felt Daniel hesitate; heard his muttered oath. But when she urged him on in a trembling whisper, he groaned and gave in to the raging need that would not wait. His hips drove forward, faster and faster, building a storm within her that exceeded the fury of the elements outside. Until at last it exploded, again and again, like a fireworks display gone wild. And in the midst of it all, she felt, deep inside her, the pulsing heat of Daniel's release.

Long moments passed as they lay together gasping, shivering and spent. Kerith was drifting dangerously close to slumber when Daniel's quietly accusing inquiry came. "How the hell did a woman as beautiful and sophisticated as you manage to keep her virginity this long? And why didn't you warn me?"

6

RAIN LASHED FURIOUSLY against the windows of Daniel's living room, and a heavy boom of thunder echoed in the distance, but Kerith barely heard as a sweet lethargy dragged her toward oblivion. She couldn't remember ever feeling so peaceful, so content, so . . . complete. Daniel's weight shifted against her as he propped himself on his elbows. She forced her eyes open drowsily and found him watching her expectantly.

"Are you going to tell me?" he prompted, when she didn't speak. "At this point, I think I have a right to know."

The undeniably possessive note in his voice sounded a warning deep in Kerith's mind, but she felt too good to worry about anything at the moment. "I did tell you I wasn't very experienced," she said, smiling slightly. Did everyone feel this wonderful after sex? If so, it might just be worth the risk of all the emotional entanglements that seemed to accompany the act.

"That hardly covered the issue," Daniel retorted gruffly. "I could have—" He frowned, and framed her face with his hands. "Did I hurt you? I must have. Damn, why didn't you tell me?" His obvious distress sent an unexpected wave of tenderness through Kerith, and she reached up to smooth the lines of concern furrowing his brow.

"It wasn't that bad—just an instant really. And then it was fantastic." She lowered her eyelids, shivering in remembrance. "Maybe just a little scary at the end. I felt like I was shattering into a million pieces."

Daniel's deep chuckle vibrated against her breasts, as he bent to nibble gently on her earlobe. "It was fantastic, wasn't it? In fact, I'm still shaking from it."

He wasn't exaggerating. Kerith could feel the fine vibration everywhere their bodies touched. It gave her a gratifying sense of power. "Does that always happen?"

Daniel levered himself up again to smile down at her. "No. I've never felt anything like this. It's almost like a madness. I used to pride myself in being a slow, considerate lover, but the way I just treated you was closer to a neanderthal's tactics."

"Hey, quit punishing yourself. I told you I loved it." She stretched experimentally, then froze when she realized he was still inside her, and still very much aroused. "Um...are you...? I mean, I thought I felt..." Words failed her.

"Yes I did, and yes I still am," Daniel supplied, punctuating each word with a light kiss. "Once wasn't nearly enough, with you. However, before we start discussing an encore, there's a more serious subject that needs to be addressed, and that's your protection—or lack of it. I assume you aren't using any form of birth control. And I, in the heat of the moment, forgot for the first time since I was a reckless teenager." He used a fingertip to trace the elegant line of her cheekbone. "I'm sorry, Kerith. I won't be so careless again. And if anything should…happen, you don't need to worry. I'll take full responsibility."

A swift dart of alarm pierced Kerith's cloud of bliss, as the import of his last words struck home. He was talking about her becoming pregnant, about permanent consequences she wasn't prepared to consider. It couldn't happen that easily, could it? No, of course not. Most women had to try for months to get pregnant. Still, the possibility made her shift uneasily beneath Daniel's suddenly threatening weight, and she brought her hands between them to push at his chest. "Don't you think you're being a bit premature, pledging yourself to something so unlikely?" she asked irritably.

Obliging her bid for space, Daniel eased his body away to the side, but the moment he left her, Kerith wished he hadn't. An empty loneliness settled over her, and she was relieved when he pulled her around to face him on the wide cushions.

"I didn't mean to upset you, love," he said softly, his hand stroking comfortingly down her back. "I was just trying to be realistic. We don't have to think about it anymore, now."

"Perhaps you should take me home…" Kerith's voice trailed off in a moan as his caress strayed from comfort to sensuality. And the last of her unease fled as he gathered her against the inviting heat of his naked body.

"Oh no, not yet," he implored softly. "I have a lot of making up to do." He slipped one hand down to cup the damp curls shielding her femininity, and she immediately quivered in response. "If you're too sore to have me inside again, I know lots of other ways to love you.

In fact, I probably won't have enough time in one night to demonstrate all of them."

He slipped off the couch and scooped her up, robe and all. "Come on, I want to show you what an attractive bedroom I have."

As Daniel crossed the darkened living room and started up a curved staircase, Kerith wrapped her arms around his neck and gave herself up to the delicious lure of returning passion. After all, what difference did it make at this point if she stayed the night? The risk had already been taken, she might as well get as much pleasure as possible out of it. Consequences could be dealt with tomorrow.

WHEN KERITH WOKE the next morning it was with a sense of disorientation. Wondering why her bed felt different, she stirred restlessly beneath unfamiliar blue sheets, and the soreness at the juncture of her thighs brought instant recall. This was Daniel's bed. And last night they had . . . Groaning softly, she turned onto her stomach and buried her face in the pillow.

"That bad, hmm?" Daniel's voice came from somewhere nearby, and when she whipped her head around to look, she found him seated on the edge of the bed, steaming mugs of coffee in his hands. "I warned you that last time would be too much."

"It's very ungentlemanly of you to remind me," Kerith complained, lowering her face to the pillow again. The memory of what he'd done to her—what she'd done to him!—inspired an urge to bury herself under the covers completely. And when she peered at him from behind the tawny disarray of her hair, she discovered a more disquieting side effect of the night before. A strange thrill stirred in the depths of her heart; not unlike the feeling one experienced at the top of an dangerously steep ski run right before pushing off. In skiing, she'd relished the sensation. Now, she found it vaguely frightening.

"I brought you café au lait," Daniel announced placatingly. "Will that redeem me?" He set the mugs down and propped two fluffy pillows against the headboard, then settled himself there. "I also think you look absolutely beautiful in the morning."

"Your eyesight must have deteriorated overnight," Kerith quipped, but the heady aroma of freshly brewed coffee overcame her reticence. Gingerly, she scooted up next to him, the sheet carefully clasped to her breasts.

Daniel had reclaimed his robe, and she had to admit it looked far better on him. Even with his hair rumpled and his face unshaven, he looked marvelous. While she, on the other hand, probably resembled a tornado victim. Accepting the mug he offered, she sipped and let out a reluctant hum of appreciation. "No one ever served me coffee in bed before."

"Not even Gus?"

Kerith sighed and rested the mug on her lap. She'd wondered how long it would be before that subject came up. Her eyes moved restlessly over the masculine oak furniture in Daniel's tastefully decorated bedroom. It was definitely a man's room. And Daniel was going to want to know why his was the first man's bed she'd slept in.

"Tell me about your marriage, Kerith. Tell me why I was the first, instead of your husband."

"Gus was a very special man," she began hesitantly. "He sort of adopted me when he found out I was an orphan. Then he discovered he had terminal cancer, and since he didn't have any living relatives, he decided I should be the one to inherit his business. Legal adoption would have been complicated, since my birth records were incomplete and registered in a foreign country. So he suggested a platonic marriage."

"Did you know he was dying when you married him?"

"Of course not!" She shot him hurt look. "What kind of woman do you think I am? He told me he was impotent—that I didn't have to worry about any demands for a physical relationship between us. But I didn't find out the cause was cancer until months after the wedding."

"Did you love him? Is that why you married him?"

Kerith closed her eyes against the pain his question brought. "No. I did it because he offered companionship and security—two things I'd never known—with no strings attached. He told me he wanted to be sure the business would be in good hands if anything ever happened to him, and I didn't allow myself to question his motives. I knew I didn't want a traditional marriage, and what he offered sounded good at the time. What I didn't count on was the depth of his feelings for me." She twisted her fingers into the folds of the sheet. "Sometimes I wish I could have..." Suddenly aware she was again revealing too much of herself, she turned away and set her mug on the night table on her side of the wide bed. "I think it's time for me to go. Would you get my things? I'm sure they're dry now."

"Not so fast." Daniel's arm wrapped around her waist, pulling her back. "What about the others?"

"What others?" She began to struggle ineffectually, as he slid down in the bed and snuggled their bodies together, her back hard up against his chest, her bottom nestled against—No, don't start thinking about that again, she ordered herself sternly, even as her mind was filled with vivid memories of the night before.

"I mean, all the other men in the world who saw you and wanted to make love to you. Why didn't any of them succeed?"

"Because..." Kerith drew a quick breath as his mouth brushed softly over her nape and down her shoulder, leaving a rapidly spreading trail of heat. "Because...I never...wanted...Oh, don't do that."

"What? This?" He tugged her over until she lay on her back, his tongue flicking out to taste the delicate skin of her throat. "So sweet, like honey and cream. Did I tell you how much I love to taste you?"

"Daniel, please stop," Kerith whispered faintly, her resistance slipping. She might have lost it completely if the phone on Daniel's side of the bed hadn't shrilled just then, startling them both. Daniel hesitated, obviously ready to ignore it, but on the third ring he gave in and reached for the receiver, swearing succinctly.

Kerith scrambled off the other side of the bed, dragging the sheet with her to use as a makeshift cover as she went in search of her clothes. The intrusion of the phone had served to remind her of the real world, with all its problems and complications, waiting for her outside the fantasy world she'd been living in since last night. And the biggest complication was, she actually felt reluctant to leave.

As she carefully navigated the stairs she told herself that nothing had changed. She'd had sex with the man, but she was still the same woman.

She stubbed her toe on the bottom step and swore. Who was she kidding? Everything had changed. Who would have guessed satisfying a simple physical urge could have such a strong emotional effect? It didn't happen every time. Not if the current popularity of one-night stands was any indication. So why did she feel as if Daniel Avanti had invaded not only her body, but her very soul? Every time she'd looked at him this morning, there'd been a scary tightening in the region of her heart.

Kerith's anxiety deepened to frustration as she searched fruitlessly for her clothing. There was no evidence of the missing articles in Daniel's neat, compact kitchen, nor were they in the adjoining dining area, which looked out over an inner courtyard and pool shared by Daniel and his immediate neighbors. Outside, the sun was shining brilliantly, as if the previous night's storm had been an illusion. But the clear brilliance of the sky didn't lighten Kerith's mood. Instead, a premonition of doom clouded over her, making her steps quicken with determination as she headed back toward the living room.

Daniel arrived at the bottom of the stairs just as she swept into the room. In one large hand, he held a hangar containing her dress, in the other was clutched her frilly underwear. Kerith felt something in her stomach give way. The hand that held those silky intimate articles so casually had known her with equal intimacy. How would she ever be able to forget that?

"You were looking for these?" he said, smiling.

"Yes, thank you." She hurried over and practically snatched her things from him. "I'd like to get dressed now."

"What's the rush?" Daniel inquired, bending to pluck the dragging ends of the sheet out of her way as she stumbled on up the stairs.

She didn't answer until she'd reached the door of the bathroom separating the two upstairs bedrooms. "I'm sure you must have things to do on your day off, as I do." She turned, deliberately blocking the doorway.

"As a matter of fact, I do. That was my sister on the phone, reminding me of my mother's birthday party this afternoon."

"Well then, I'd better hurry and change so you can take me home." She stepped into the bathroom and started to close the door in his face, but he pushed it open and followed her inside, his expression suddenly grim.

"If you don't mind, I'd like some privacy—" she began sharply, but he cut her off.

"Stop it, Kerith." There was an unsettling determination in his expression as he started toward her, and Kerith backed away until she bumped into the far wall.

"Stop what?"

The sheet had slipped a little and he caught her bare shoulders in a firm grip and gave her a little shake. "Stop acting as if last night was just a casual encounter, something you're going to walk away from without a second thought."

She refused to look at his face, staring instead at the tanned vee of hairy chest exposed by his robe. "Why should that bother you? It's what you're used to, isn't it?" It was a low blow, one she regretted the moment the words were out. But just looking at his chest made her feel week-kneed and far too vulnerable.

His fingers tightened painfully. "Dammit, Kerith, that was unfair. I told you how much you mean to me. Hell, I'm even tempted to skip that birthday party today, just so I can be alone with you a little longer. Considering I haven't been home for my mother's birthday in over ten years, I think that's pretty significant."

She threw her head back, prepared to meet the anger in his face, but instead she saw a combination of hurt and frustration that pulled at her heart. "I'm sorry, Daniel," she whispered, turning her head away. "But I think we both would have been better off if last night hadn't happened."

Daniel's hands relaxed, and he gently caught her chin and made her look into his eyes. "You're wrong, love. And I can prove it, if you'll just give me the chance."

"I don't want to become involved with you," she insisted, as he brushed his mouth tenderly across her forehead. Just that simple caress made her body start to go soft and languid.

"But you already are." His lips teased hers with the lightest of plucking kisses, until she tilted her head searching for more.

And, heaven help her, she knew he was right. When he wrapped his arms around her, she gave a small moan of resignation. "It'll never work," she protested uselessly, as his familiar manly scent tugged at her senses.

"Trust me. Stay with me today."

"What about your mother's party?"

"Go with me."

Alarm made her stiffen momentarily. "I couldn't. I abhor family gatherings. Too much noise and confusion."

"Please, Kerith. For me?" Daniel's fingertips began to coax the tension out of her back.

"I'll be terrible company," she threatened, but her resolve was weakening again.

"Let me worry about that." This time when he kissed her, there was no teasing, just a seductive need. By the time their lips parted, she couldn't bring herself to deny him anything.

"All right, I'll go."

His hug nearly squeezed the breath out of her. "You won't regret it," he assured her, his smile dazzling.

But he was wrong, she thought a while later, watching him draw a hot bath to soothe her morning-after aches. She regretted it already.

By the time they arrived at Rosa Avanti's comfortable ranch-style house that afternoon, Kerith's regret had darkened to a sense of foreboding. As a result, a headache had formed at the base of her skull, and it worsened when they went inside. The place was packed to the walls with laughing, shouting, gesticulating people. Worse yet, once in their midst, Daniel seemed to transform into one of them.

Kerith was jostled on every side as Daniel tugged her through the throng, introducing her to so many people in rapid succession that names and faces became a blur.

Within five minutes her smile felt frozen in place and her headache had become a distinct throb of misery.

She wondered dismally how she could have allowed herself to be talked into this, as Daniel exchanged personal quips and joked with his relatives. Even amid the chaos she could sense a cohesiveness, a thread of unity that proclaimed them a family. And she didn't belong.

All her life she had known she was different, set apart by her lack of family, but she'd never felt it more keenly. Anger worsened the pounding discomfort in her head. She was angry at Daniel for talking her into coming, and at herself for giving in to him.

The final straw came when he introduced her to his mother. Rosa Avanti's smile was gracious as she welcomed Kerith, but her dark brown eyes—so like Daniel's—sharpened perceptibly when he mentioned Classique Limousine. "Yes, I remember now," she said slowly. "You were married to Gus Anders. My late husband thought a lot of him. We were sorry to hear of his untimely death." Her hand was warm and firm when she offered it, but the look Rosa sent her son asked a multitude of questions.

"That's very kind of you," Kerith responded, feeling as if she'd just been tried and convicted. The woman was obviously wondering what her son was doing with a known gold digger like Gus Anders's widow. Fueled by a flush of embarrassment, the heat of Kerith's anger went up several degrees. She felt as if she were steaming beneath the white linen suit she'd put on when Daniel had taken her home to change. Her headache grew to migraine proportions, and only pride kept her from marching out right then.

She persevered another hour and a half, responding only when spoken to, wishing she were anyplace else in the world—or the universe. Finally, she told Daniel she had to leave.

"What is it, love?" He had to speak directly into her ear to be heard over a stereo, which had added the music of an Italian opera to the din. "You look a little pale."

"I have a headache," she said, holding her anger at bay. She didn't want to fight with him; she wanted to get away from him.

Daniel was instantly concerned. "It's probably hunger. You didn't eat much of the omelet I fixed for you this morning. Why don't you have some dinner? I think they're about ready to serve."

The thought of food sent Kerith's stomach into a tailspin. "No, please. I just want to go home."

Daniel hesitated, the inner battle of his loyalties apparent in his distressed expression.

"Look, you don't have to leave," Kerith offered stiffly. "I'll call a cab."

"No, you won't." Daniel swore under his breath. "Just wait here a minute. I should explain to my mother." He started across the crowded room, his progress slowed by numerous affectionate bids for his attention.

There certainly wasn't any question over the prodigal's welcome, Kerith thought impatiently. How could he possibly understand her aversion to all of this? Even when he'd purposely distanced himself from his family, he must have known subconsciously he would return someday.

As Daniel started back toward her a few minutes later, Kerith eyed him critically. He looked as if he'd just stepped out of the pages of a men's fashion magazine. His navy blazer and gray slacks fit perfectly, and the pale peach shirt, casually open at the throat, was a compelling accent to his dark handsomeness. To her surprise, however, she discovered her reaction to him wasn't as overpowering, when filtered through a haze of pain and resentment.

They didn't speak as he escorted her to the gleaming black Pontiac Firebird he used for everyday driving. Kerith sank gratefully into the bucket seat and, closing her eyes, let her head drop back against the headrest. She heard Daniel get in and start the powerful engine, but the car remained parked. When she opened her eyes to determine the reason, Daniel was studying her with a frown.

Kerith sighed, and shut her eyes again. "Can we go now?"

"Of course." His response was clipped, and the tires squealed a bit as he started the car down the street. "Are you going to explain to me what came over you back there?"

"I told you, I have a headache."

"Correction: you have a headache as a result of the way you reacted to the situation at my mother's house."

"I told you I can't abide the noise and confusion of family gatherings."

"It isn't that simple, and you know it. You were chilling over, pulling in on yourself even before we got there. You prepared yourself to be miserable."

Kerith's eyes popped open in surprise. The man actually sounded angry with her. How did he dare, when it was all his fault? "I'd challenge any sane person to have a good time in that zoo."

The car jerked forward as Daniel hit the gas with unnecessary force. He was visibly upset, and it became evident he'd lost control of his temper when he spoke. "Are you jealous of my family, Kerith? Are contempt and withdrawal your way of dealing with the fact that you never had one?"

His assessment of her motives was so devastatingly accurate, Kerith felt as if she'd been laid wide open for all the world to see. Her own temper at last broke free. "Yes, damn you. It's called survival. I didn't choose the circumstances of my birth, but I learned to live with them. I was perfectly happy until you started trying to change things."

"You call that living? No emotional ties, no commitment, no love? You may have laid down those rules for Gus when you agreed to marry him, but I won't settle for them."

"No one asked you to." Kerith pressed her fingertips to her aching temples. "In fact, you won't have to put up with me at all after today."

"Like hell I won't," Daniel snapped, but he didn't argue further. A depressing silence reigned, until he'd brought the car to an abrupt halt in the driveway of Kerith's brick-and-stucco home. He sat rigid for a moment, his hands locked on the steering wheel, then his shoulders slumped and he twisted in the seat to look at her. "I'm sorry," he said in a low voice. "That got way out of control. Blame it on my Italian temper."

"I don't want to lay blame anywhere," Kerith responded dully. "I just want to be left alone." The few minutes of quiet had given her time to regain some of her composure. Now, she only wanted to put the entire episode behind her. "Goodbye, Daniel." She reached for the door handle, but his hand intercepted hers.

"Wait. I can't let you go until we have this settled."

"It is settled. I don't want to see you again. Ever."

"No, I won't accept that."

"You'll have to, because I really am too ill to argue with you anymore." She pushed his hand out of the way and opened the door, then glanced back to let him see her misery. "If you have any compassion at all, you'll leave and let me take care of my headache."

"At least let me see you to your door," he implored, as she slipped out of the car.

"No." She said it with a finality that stated clearly just how much his angry outburst was going to cost him.

Daniel felt a little sick himself as he watched Kerith disappear inside her front door. How could they have reached this point so quickly after their glorious lovemaking of the night before? He shook his head in despair, backed the car into the street and floored the gas pedal, leaving a trial of rubber that would have made any teenager proud.

After only a block, however, he backed off and proceeded at a more sedate speed. "A teenager," he muttered to himself in disgust. That was about the level of maturity he'd shown, blowing up at Kerith instead of offering understanding and support. He loved her. His entire being had been singing with the knowledge from the moment she'd welcomed him into her body with such sweet, hot fervor. The problem was, making love to her hadn't broken down the heavy walls of defense she'd erected over the years. If anything, it had probably strengthened them, because she now knew the utter vulnerability one experienced at the moment of climax.

If only he could tell her how much he loved her. But that wasn't possible, not until the business with Edelweiss was finished. He didn't want any shadow of deception between Kerith and himself when he confessed his love.

Edelweiss, Daniel thought with sudden venom, as he braked for a traffic signal. There was the real culprit in this whole mess. Why hadn't he heard anything about the proposed meeting? His mouth tightened in determination. Perhaps a call to Lucretia would speed things up in that quarter.

THE CLOCK on the dingy wall of the all-night drugstore read 10:45, as Daniel punched out a long-distance number on the pay phone. He propped one shoulder against the wall, using the other to hold the receiver to his ear. Warily he scanned his surroundings. The place appeared deserted, except for the overweight, frizzy-haired woman behind the cash register. Old habits die hard, he thought wearily, as he listened to the series of clicks routing his call. At one point, a flat, anonymous voice came on the line, demanding identification. When Daniel gave it, there were more switching noises, then Lucretia's voice, raspy with sleep.

"This had better be important, Casanova. Standard procedure is to call during normal business hours, and it's not quite three in the morning here."

Wicked satisfaction brought a smile to Daniel's face, as he automatically hunched over the phone for privacy. Even small moments of revenge could be sweet. "I was . . . uh, tied up earlier." Facing the rabid curiosity of my relatives, he added silently. There had been a minor inquisition waiting, when he'd returned to his mother's party without Kerith.

"What I want to know is when I can expect some action from Edelweiss. I've got a situation of my own to handle, and I need to get this assignment out of the way."

"What kind of situation could be urgent enough to justify dragging me out of bed?" Lucretia demanded crossly.

"Something personal. It doesn't concern you."

"It does if it involves the Anders woman. As I recall, you accepted this assignment out of concern for her as a business associate. Has that concern taken on more intimate aspects?"

Daniel ground his teeth in annoyance. He'd forgotten just how intuitive Lucretia could be. Quick, evasive action was required if he didn't want her to gain the upper hand. "You seem to have forgotten my mode of operation," he said coolly. "I don't get involved."

"There's always a first time. However, considering the lady's reputation as a cold fish, I'm inclined to believe you this time."

Kerith cold? Daniel nearly choked on that one. After last night, he couldn't imagine the word cold applying to her, in any context. "Could we get to the information I want, then?" he inquired, injecting just the right note of bored sarcasm.

"You probably won't like it. Evidently there've been more complications. No one's giving any details, but it looks like the whole project is shelved for at least a month, maybe more."

"What?" Daniel's exclamation echoed in the silent store, and when he glanced at the cashier she was staring at him nervously. He turned back to the phone, and lowered his voice to an angry murmur. "Who the hell do these guys think they are?"

"This isn't exactly a time-clock type of business, as you should know. You've handled delays before."

"That was before I had a real life to live. I don't like this. I don't like it at all."

"I could assign someone else," Lucretia suggested slyly.

Daniel barely kept himself from shouting "No!" That's all he needed, someone else from Lucretia's department messing things up. "I doubt they'd get to first base," he said, keeping his voice even. "I'm in, and I'll stay in. But I'd appreciate it if you'd light a fire under these people. And while you're at it, you might tell this Edelweiss character not to be too surprised if his welcoming committee isn't too enthusiastic. The lady has some bad memories involving the name."

"I'm not among the privileged who speak to Edelweiss, but I'll pass it along," Lucretia agreed, her tone implying she couldn't see any point in doing so.

"Good. I'll be waiting to hear from you." He paused and added meaningfully, "Let's hope it's soon." He hung up with barely restrained force, and strode toward the door.

On the way, he passed a row of Las Vegas's ubiquitous slot machines, and on a whim he stopped and fished in one pocket for a quarter. It clinked cheerfully, when he pushed it into the coin slot and pulled on the handle. The triple display spun into a blur, then clicked three figures into place—a lemon, an orange and a cherry. Useless. A big zero. Daniel made a disgusted sound and continued out the door, his hands shoved into his pockets. Luck seemed to be running full tilt against him today. Heaven help him, if it didn't improve when he tried to redeem himself with Kerith.

7

"YOU LOOK LIKE you were bitten by the same flu bug that had me under the weather all weekend." Ali Spencer stood in the doorway to Kerith's office and scrutinized her employer with a critical eye. "Is that the reason you left Rosa Avanti's party so abruptly?"

Kerith looked up from the accounting statement she'd been checking. Her mouth quirked in annoyance as she gestured for Ali to have a seat. "Who told you I was at the party?"

"Rosa did, when I called to apologize for not making it myself. She said you were with Daniel." Ali strolled over and draped herself elegantly in one of the turquoise chairs facing Kerith's desk. "Does this have anything to do with the reason you weren't home to answer your phone Friday night?" Uncertainty suddenly furrowed Ali's brow. "Or am I overstepping again by asking that?"

Kerith sighed and leaned back in her chair. "I'll tell you, but only because I want you to understand why the subject of Daniel Avanti is off-limits around here."

"Oh brother, this doesn't sound good."

"It was an unfortunate set of circumstances," Kerith corrected, tiredly massaging the back of her neck. Saturday's headache was only a faint echo now, but tension had taken up permanent residence in her shoulders. "Daniel and I took the Rolls out for a test run Friday night and got stranded in the storm."

Ali barely suppressed a smile. "The Duchess is still up to her old tricks, hmm?"

"With a vengeance. Daniel's brother-in-law rescued us and dropped us both at Daniel's place, since it was storming too hard to risk any unnecessary driving with the Rolls in tow. When Daniel invited me to wait out the storm with him, I agreed." Kerith dropped her gaze and felt a slight flush warm her face. She'd intended to come across sophisticated and nonchalant about the whole thing, but apparently some subjects didn't automatically become easier with age. "It was a big mistake."

"You weren't . . . um, compatible?"

Ali's delicately posed inquiry made Kerith look up. Her friend's green eyes were filled with a gentle concern that put to rest any question of prurient interest, but there was a limit to what Kerith could bring herself to reveal. "Daniel Avanti and I come from totally different backgrounds," she said evasively. "Even if I were interested in having a relationship, it wouldn't work."

Ali drew a deep breath and let it out slowly. "Sometimes differences have a way of working themselves out, when genuine caring is involved. I think Daniel cares for you a great deal."

Kerith's newfound resolve tightened instinctively. Somewhere in the wee hours of Sunday morning, after a night of tormented soul-searching, she'd decided on a method of overcoming her susceptibility to Daniel. "I don't want our differences solved," she said resolutely. "In fact, I don't intend to see Mr. Avanti again, except when business makes it unavoidable."

"But—" The buzzing of the intercom interrupted Ali's protest.

"Mr. Avanti is here to see you," Charlotte announced cheerfully.

Kerith groaned softly. She'd been half expecting this, but now that the moment was here she couldn't bring herself to face it. "Tell him I'm not in."

"He already knows you are. He said to tell you he'd sit out here all day if necessary." Charlotte's voice lowered to an excited whisper. "He has roses, at least two dozen of them. They're absolutely gorgeous."

Realizing it would be better to face him now and get it over, Kerith gave in and told Charlotte to send him in. But when Daniel appeared in the open doorway, the force of her reaction dismayed her. Her pulse doubled, and within the depths of her being there was a shudder of recognition. The man had been her lover, even if for only one night, and it appeared she wouldn't be able to forget it quickly.

Kerith rose, thankful for the man-tailored rust suit she'd chosen to wear that day. It gave her a badly needed sense of fortification against the feminine weakness Daniel engendered. "Good morning, Mr. Avanti," she said with amazing composure. "How may I help you?"

At mention of Daniel's name, Ali was out of her chair like a shot and heading for the door. "Hi, Daniel. I was just leaving."

"There's no need," Kerith protested sharply. "I'm sure our business will be brief." But Ali was already zipping out the door, pulling it shut behind her.

"I guess she must be aware of what's going on between us," Daniel observed, smiling slightly.

As he moved toward her desk, however, Kerith saw that his handsome features were marred by fatigue. She stiffened every muscle in her body, resisting a pang of sympathy. "There isn't anything between us," she replied firmly.

Ignoring her denial, Daniel positioned himself just in front of her desk. The roses—a mix of apricot and pristine white this time—lay casually in the crook of his arm, a curiously appealing accent to his gray business suit. "You didn't return the messages I left on your home answering machine. That wasn't very polite."

"It also wasn't polite to fill the entire tape with the same message," Kerith countered. "Nor is it considered good form to pound on a person's door after it's apparent she isn't going to answer."

"I didn't pound."

"Knock repeatedly, then." Kerith sighed impatiently. "There isn't any point to this conversation. I told you I don't want to see you again. Why don't you accept that?"

"Because I can't." Pain flashed in the deep brown of Daniel's eyes. "And I don't believe you will, either, once you've gotten over being angry with me." He held out the roses, but she refused to take them, so he lay them on the desk, a fragrant peace offering.

"Anger isn't the issue," Kerith began, picking up the flowers and practically tossing them into his arms.

"I know. It's trust. And I betrayed yours badly when I selfishly forced you into a situation you weren't prepared to handle. I'm truly sorry for that, Kerith."

"I don't want your apologies. I want to be left alone."

Daniel shook his head almost regretfully. "That isn't possible anymore. You and I belong together; Friday night convinced me of that. Now all I have to do is convince you."

Frustration at his persistence caused Kerith's temper to erupt. "To put it in your words, 'That isn't possible.' Now, will you please leave and not come back?"

Daniel sighed unhappily. "I knew this wouldn't be easy. All right, I'll go, for now. But I'll be back. I won your trust once, and I believe I can win it again." He leaned forward and stroked her soft cheek before she could flinch away, then turned and left with a self-confident spring to his step that provoked her further.

"Stay away from me, Daniel Avanti," she warned fiercely. If he heard her, he gave no indication of it, but in the weeks that followed, it appeared he had, because she didn't actually see him more than once or twice. Which didn't mean he'd absented himself from her life. On the contrary, hardly a day passed without some contact, however subtle.

He began sending her a rose every day, which she promptly threw in the trash. But when Charlotte bemoaned the waste and pleaded for permission to keep the rejected blossoms in a vase on her own desk, Kerith relented a little and agreed.

Then there was the expensive espresso machine, delivered to Classique Limousine with a generous supply of gourmet coffee. That gift would have been sent back immediately, but Charlotte unknowingly unpacked it in the employee lounge, and the delight it generated in the morning assembly there seemed to preclude grand gestures on Kerith's part. Anyway, she reasoned defensively, if the man wanted to waste his money making her employees happy, he could go right ahead. It wouldn't have any influence on her feelings—as long as she didn't allow herself to think about cappuccino. And she still had the power to refuse to see him or accept his telephone calls.

When the notes began appearing, however, the situation wasn't quite as simple. The first one she found in mid-September, tucked in the visor of her car after it had been to Avanti's for regular servicing. Until that time, Kerith had considered maintaining business relations with Daniel to be a sign of her total disregard for what had passed between them. Aside from that, reputation-wise he was the only game in town when it came to keeping her fleet of limousines operational. But when she read the note he'd written, she began to wish there were other options.

Daniel's heavy, masculine scrawl nearly filled the small slip of paper. "I remember how lovely your golden body looked by firelight, and I ache."

Kerith closed her eyes and felt the heat of that fire sweep through her body as surely as if she'd still been lying before the flickering flames. Damn it! She should be over the whole thing by now. Why this lingering weakness?

She opened her eyes and glared at the spot where the note had been hidden. He must have put it there before his mechanic returned the car.... A new outrage occurred to her, and she scrambled out of the car and ran back to her office.

"Damn you, Daniel Avanti," she snapped, as soon as his secretary had routed the call to his office. "I don't wish to be the subject of your... your pornography. Especially when you leave it lying around for all the world to see."

"Kerith, love, how nice to hear your voice," Daniel responded, pleasure reverberating in each word. "If I'd known writing a note would do the trick, I'd have tried it sooner."

"What trick? Embarrassing me in front of your employees? Making me the topic of their shop gossip?"

"What are you talking about?" Daniel sounded more confused than happy now.

"Your mechanic, the one who picked up my car this morning and returned it this afternoon. How could you leave a note like that where he could find it?" The very idea made her stomach churn, something it had been doing with little provocation lately. She sat down at her desk and glared out the west window, totally unappreciative of the magnificent sunset gilding the distant mountainous horizon. Why did she feel so lousy all the time, lately? It was barely six o'clock, and she was exhausted already. Daniel's relieved laughter made her feel worse.

"Relax love, no one saw the note. I drove your car back this afternoon. I tried to see you, but as usual, your secretary said you were unavailable. Do you think it's fair to use her as a shield between us? The poor woman looks utterly miserable every time she has to lie to me." He hesitated, sighed, then went on in a more subdued tone. "I still want you Kerith, more than ever. Won't you give me another chance?"

The naked longing in his plea stirred an unwilling response in the depths of her soul, but she quickly suppressed it. "I learned a long time ago that wanting something doesn't necessarily make it happen. Don't you think it's time you accepted that fact, too?" She didn't wait for his answer. The ivory receiver hit its resting place with considerable force as she hung up. The incoming line on Charlotte's extension began to ring almost immediately, but Charlotte was gone for the day, and Kerith didn't give the clamoring instrument a second glance as she passed on her way out.

SEPTEMBER CAME and went in a blaze of scorching days that made it seem as if Mother Nature were bent on compensating for the relative mildness of August. Adding noticeably to the heat, were Daniel's notes, which continued to appear mysteriously in places only Kerith would find them: her purse, her locked desk drawer, the pocket of her suit jacket. Some were unabashedly erotic, reminding her vividly of their night together. Others had an emotional poignancy that almost frightened her. Strangely enough, the latter were the ones she began saving first—although after a while she found herself stowing even the 'hot' ones in the small, locked chest where she kept her jewelry. In the beginning, she told herself she kept the notes as a reminder of her one foray into stupidity, but after a time, a more troubling motive occurred to her. Despite all her determined efforts, there was a chink in her armor, a soft spot. And it belonged to the man who had taught her the meaning of ecstasy.

OCTOBER BROUGHT cooling temperatures, and a sigh of relief from everyone at Classique Limousine. The milder weather sparked a general vivacity among Kerith's employees that made her more aware of the fatigue and general listlessness that continued to plague her. Hoping it was nothing more than a simple case of anemia, she made an appointment with her physician. When she left his office on a balmy day in mid-October, she knew her life course had been permanently altered.

"YOU'RE PREGNANT!" Ali popped to a sitting position on the chaise lounge from which she'd been dreamily contemplating a bright orange Halloween moon.

"Shh! Not so loud." Kerith sat forward on the webbed patio chair she'd been using and glanced nervously toward the sliding glass door leading to Ali's house. They were alone on the patio, but only two rooms away Ali's daughter was counting her trick-or-treat candy and watching a horror movie on the living-room television. With her was their neighbor, Sam, a somber bearded giant totally unlike Ali's usual boyfriends. Ali had been seeing Sam a lot lately, a surprising turnaround in her social habits. He had a quiet, easy way with little Cami that Kerith found reassuring, but that didn't mean she wanted to share her life's secrets with him. Telling Ali had been hard enough.

"This isn't a public announcement," she cautioned in a whisper. "I only told you because..." Kerith turned her head away abruptly and faced the dark expanse of Ali's backyard. "Because I just needed to tell someone. I haven't even decided what I'm going to do yet."

"Does that mean you're considering an abortion?" Ali asked in a low voice.

Kerith stiffened, her response instant and vehement. "No! Never!" The words echoed in the quiet night, as she slumped back and tilted her head to gaze at the night sky. "Adoption is out, too," she went on slowly. "I know what it's like to be unwanted."

"As I see it, that leaves you two options: marriage or single-parenting. Have you considered what Daniel's reaction will be?"

Kerith glanced at her sharply. "Why should I?"

"Oh, come on. You and I both know he's the only man you've been with lately. I think he has a right to know he's going to be a father."

"Well, I don't. And I trust you're not planning to change your hands-off policy concerning Daniel and me." Kerith jumped up and walked quickly to the edge of the concrete patio. "I guarantee, I won't be forgiving."

"I thought I'd proved myself in that area over the last few months." Ali's voice was etched with hurt.

Kerith turned back, her expression filled with regret. "I'm sorry, you didn't deserve that. Your restraint has been admirable." Wrapping her arms tightly around her waist, she moved back to her chair and sat. "You've never mentioned anything, but . . . has he ever tried to get you involved?"

Ali shook her head. "Not unless you consider an occasional phone call to ask if you're okay. Daniel may be an old friend, but he's about as closemouthed as you are, when it comes to emotions. I do think, however, that the man has fallen in love with you. If he knew about that baby you're carrying—"

"I wouldn't know a moment's peace," Kerith interrupted impatiently. "Which is precisely why I won't tell him."

"It's going to be pretty hard to hide after a few months," Ali pointed out ruefully.

"I know that." Kerith hopped up again and began to pace. "I could always tell him there had been someone else." She saw Ali's skeptically raised eyebrow. "Or I could leave Las Vegas before he knew. I'm sure I could sell Classique and start over somewhere else."

"Good grief, you'd go that far? What are you so afraid of? Daniel is a kind, honorable man. Unless I miss my guess, he probably would be happy to marry you, or at the very least share the responsibility of raising his child."

"That's the problem." Kerith stopped pacing and threw her hands out in frustration. "I don't want to get married. It's my baby, my responsibility. I don't need his help."

"Are you sure? Even though my ex-husband was a louse most of the time, I was glad to have him around when I was carrying Cami. Pregnancy can make you feel incredibly vulnerable, at times. Probably has something to do with hormones."

"You and Cami seem to have done all right since you've been on your own."

Ali got up and walked over to place one hand on Kerith's shoulder. "I thought so, too, until Sam came into my life." She cast a fond glance toward the house. "In the last few weeks he's shown me what I've been missing—what Cami's been missing, too. Companionship . . . support . . . love . . . You can survive without them, Kerith, but it isn't easy."

Kerith experienced a twinge of disappointment. Until that moment, she hadn't realized how much she'd been counting on Ali's support. Ali had always seemed to be the ultimate, liberated woman, strong enough to walk away from a destructive marriage and raise her young daughter alone, without losing the feminine warmth that made her such a good friend.

"I think I'd actually marry Sam . . . if he ever gets up the nerve to ask me," Ali continued with a wry smile. "Can you believe that, coming from me? Normally, I wouldn't hesitate to propose myself, but Sam inspires something traditional in me. I'm actually enjoying an old-fashioned courtship."

Tradition. Courtship. Marriage. Ali was beginning to sound like one of those flowery romance novels. Purposely stepping away from Ali's comforting hand, Kerith said stiffly, "If you're sure that's what you want, I'm happy for you. But don't expect me to jump on the bandwagon. I'm not like you. I don't need the things you're talking about."

"Don't you?" Ali's voice came quietly from the darkness behind Kerith. "You might find it's not so easy being self-sufficient, now that you have another life dependent on yours."

"I'll be fine," Kerith insisted, then quickly changed the subject. But only two days later something happened that made Ali's words sound prophetic.

THE COLLISION occurred in the middle of morning rush-hour traffic. Kerith never saw the other car coming. She just felt a tremendous jolt, right before the scenery started spinning. When her small sports car finally stopped, it was facing the wrong way on the other side of the busy intersection. According to the officer who appeared almost immediately, Kerith and the woman who'd broadsided her were lucky to have escaped without serious injury. Their cars weren't as fortunate.

As she surveyed the extensive damage to her RX-7, Kerith acknowledged the man's assessment with a vague nod, but the full realization of what might have happened didn't really hit her until she sat down beside her badly dented car to wait for the arrival of the tow truck.

I could have been killed, she thought. And then a heavier knowledge settled over her. Her life hadn't been the only one at risk. Another life—her unborn child—now depended on her for survival. The enormity of that responsibility made her begin to shake.

By the time she'd finished answering the police officer's questions, accompanied by the hysterical weeping of the woman who'd caused the accident, Kerith's endurance had almost run out. So when she heard a screech of tires and looked up to see Daniel's Firebird pulling up right behind his brother-in-law's tow truck, she felt relief rather than annoyance. He looked like a knight charging to the rescue as he lunged out of the car and raced toward her.

"Kerith, sweetheart, are you all right?" He crouched down in front of where she sat on the curb and took her trembling hands in his big, strong ones. "When Tom called me and said you'd been in an accident, I thought my heart would stop. Do you need a doctor? Have they called an ambulance?"

"I don't need an ambulance," she assured him quickly, the shaking already beginning to subside. "But the officer said I'll probably have a nasty bruise from the shoulder harness on the seat belt. And he suggested I see my doctor, just to make sure everything is all right."

"I'll take you as soon as you're finished here."

"You . . . you don't have to do that. I'm sure someone will come for me as soon as I contact my office."

"Not a chance, honey. I'm not letting you out of my sight until I know you're really okay. Now, do you feel up to walking, or should I carry you to the car?"

Kerith hastily opted for walking, but she couldn't talk him out of driving her to the doctor's office. Nor could she stop him from waiting for her there.

The doctor was encouraging. "You don't seem to have any serious injuries, although that seat-belt bruise may be a little tender for a while." He gave her a reassuring smile. "And you don't have to worry about your baby. Mother Nature does a pretty good job of protecting the little rascals. Just call me if you notice anything unusual."

When Kerith returned to the waiting room, Daniel was restlessly leafing through a magazine, and the worry in his eyes, when he looked up, gave her a moment's pause. How much deeper would that concern be if he knew of the child she carried? His child. Guilt nibbled at the edge of her conscience, but she quickly pushed it away. She couldn't afford such feelings. For that matter, allowing him just this small contact had been a mistake.

But Daniel wasn't so easily dismissed. He drove her to work, then insisted she keep the Firebird. "One of your drivers can drop me off at my place," he explained when she resisted. "Your car is going to need quite a bit of repair work, and Avanti's does provide loaners occasionally."

Kerith frowned and crossed her arms over her midriff as she leaned against the Firebird's gleaming fender. "But this is your car. What will you drive?"

"My Jag. I've been intending to use it more, now that the weather has cooled down."

"Daniel, I can't let you do this. It doesn't feel right after... after what happened." It also didn't feel right to have her heart tripping along at a dangerous clip just because he was standing so close and looking so damned attractive. Was there another man alive who had such meltingly dark brown eyes?

"There's no law against being nice," he said, a certain sadness clouding his gaze. "At least allow me that, Kerith."

Reluctantly, she agreed, thinking it would be easier to return the car later, when its disturbing owner wasn't around. A few nights later, however, she found herself heading for the Firebird yet again as she crossed the darkened employee's parking lot. "Face it, you enjoy driving the thing," she muttered to herself. But it went deeper than that, and she knew it. In truth, she was hooked on sliding into the deep bucket seat and inhaling the lingering scent of Daniel's aftershave. Anticipation of indulging herself again had her so preoccupied, she didn't notice Arthur lounging on the front fender until he spoke.

"Your Italian friend must think a lot of you, letting you use his car all this time."

Kerith's head jerked around as she paused, one hand on the Firebird's door handle. "Arthur! For heaven's sake, what are you doing lurking around out here? You nearly scared me to death."

"Sorry. I was merely enjoying a moment of fresh air." Arthur smiled apologetically and strolled closer, until he was so near she could smell the acrid licorice of the imported lozenges he favored. The scent nauseated her slightly, so she opened the car door and stepped behind it to put some distance between them. The man still made her uneasy, and lately there had been an intensity in his eyes when he looked at her that added to her wariness. His overtures toward her had remained casual and friendly, but the last few times she'd turned him down, his polite acceptance had seemed to mask a far more emotional response. His next words seemed to justify her suspicions. "You've been seeing a lot of that Avanti fellow lately." Arthur's smile twisted almost to a grimace. "Who would have dreamed you'd have a weakness for the Latin-lover type?"

His vehemence surprised Kerith into defending herself. "I don't have a weakness for anyone, Latin or otherwise, but I do think you have a lot of nerve calling names considering the number of rich, lonely ladies you currently have on a string."

"Hardly the same thing. Those women are old, no longer attractive. I'm merely being kind to them because no one else will. You're different, Kerith. You deserve a man who will take care of you; someone you can trust. Avanti could never be that for you, but I could."

The man's taken leave of his senses, Kerith thought. *And he couldn't be more wrong.* If she were inclined to trust any man again, it would be Daniel. He had proved his concern for her welfare and happiness repeatedly, without any encouragement from her. And while she still considered her brief venture into intimacy a mistake, she had to admit she couldn't imagine any man, other than Daniel, being able to tempt her to try it in the first place. Yet, here was Arthur, thinking himself the answer to her lonely widow's prayers. She couldn't stop an incredulous smile as she regarded his slightly condescending expression. "Arthur this is . . . absurd. I don't need anyone to take care of me."

Even in the dim light, she could see the disastrous effect of her amusement. Arthur's angular features became like chipped granite. "You're laughing at me," he accused with sudden heat. "You're choosing him over me, after all the time I've waited . . ." Suddenly, his hands were pressing her fingers into the top edge of the door.

The look in his pale eyes reminded Kerith of a wounded animal, and though the unexpected change in his behavior made her uneasy, a spark of empathy stirred in her heart. She knew how painful rejection could be.

"Arthur, I think I should remind you of something," she said very carefully. "Even if I were in need of someone, I would never become involved with an employee."

"You're too good for me, is that it?" Arthur demanded raggedly.

Irritation overrode her compassion. "No, that is not it. And would you please let go of my hands? You're hurting me." The sharp ring of authority in her voice seemed to bring Arthur back to his senses.

He hastily released her and stepped back. When he spoke, he sounded embarrassed and contrite. "I've really overstepped, haven't I?"

"Yes, you have," Kerith agreed, relieved to be in control again. "I try to maintain a friendly relationship with my employees, but that doesn't mean I welcome unsuitable familiarity. I have no use for a chauffeur who can't remember his place, whether it's with myself or with one of the people who use my limousine service." She saw Arthur stiffen in alarm, and relented a little. "You have an excellent working record, and I'd hate to have to terminate you."

"You . . . you won't find that necessary, if . . . if you'll only give me another chance," Arthur choked out.

Realizing how hard it must be for a man like Arthur to plead, Kerith relented even further. "All right. For now, we'll consider this little incident forgotten."

He nodded and thanked her awkwardly before turning toward his own car. Watching him go, Kerith decided she'd handled the situation in the best way possible. But over the next few days, she found she couldn't quite forget it. The part about trusting Daniel came back again and again, in annoying challenge to her self-proclaimed independence.

"You don't need him or anyone else," she told herself for the hundredth time, as she unlocked her front door late Saturday night. She pushed the door open, then hesitated. In the past, coming home to an empty house had never bothered her, but lately she'd been feeling edgy.

"Must be those overactive hormones Ali was talking about," she muttered, stepping inside.

The carved cuckoo clock she'd brought from Switzerland brightly announced nine o'clock as she entered the living room. She paused, savoring the homey sound, but when she turned on the light, her sense of security vanished.

Someone had been in her house! Everywhere she looked, there was evidence of the ruthless invasion. The edelweiss plant lay on its side, the lovely pot cracked in half, the soil spilling over the small table on which it had stood. Cushions lay helter-skelter, magazines and books were scattered and paintings had been pulled from the walls.

Fingers pressed to her lips to hold in a gasp, Kerith scanned the room with panic-stricken eyes. What else had they done? There! On shelves of her curio cabinet, more destruction. All the little knickknacks she'd collected over the years—so many of them depicting the edelweiss in some way—all were broken and scattered.

Who would do such a thing? Why?

The phone shrilled, startling a scream from her throat. She grabbed it and barely croaked a hello.

"Kerith? Is that you?" Daniel's deep voice wrapped around her like a comforting arm.

"Yes," she replied in a tremulous whisper. "D-daniel, some . . . someone's broken in . . ." Her voice failed.

"Kerith! I can barely hear you. What's going on?"

"They. . . they destroyed my edelweiss . . ."

"I still can't hear you. Did you say edelweiss?" His voice sharpened. "Is Edelweiss there with you?"

"N . . . no." She raised her free hand to the phone receiver and tried to think clearly. "I think—No, I *know* someone's been in my house . . ."

Daniel's startled oath cut her off. "Listen carefully, love. I want you to get out of there this minute. Don't stop for anything. Get in your car and drive to that little convenience store two blocks away. You know the one?"

"Yes." A random thought occurred to her. "What about the police? I should . . ."

"I'll take care of it. Just wait for me at the store. And lock your car doors!"

"But . . ."

"Go!" The force of that one word drove her out the front door without further hesitation.

KERITH WASN'T SURE how long she'd been waiting when Daniel drove his low-slung sports car into the parking lot of the brightly lit store, but it seemed like hours. And when he scooped her up into his warm, reassuring embrace, she knew a contentment beyond anything she'd experienced before.

"Kerith, thank God. I think I broke every speed record in the state getting here." He held her at arm's length to look her over. "Are you okay?"

She nodded, a smile pulling at her mouth as she took in his disheveled appearance. His rumpled dress shirt was unbuttoned and hanging free of his trousers, his feet were bare, and he'd never looked better to her. "You could have taken the time to put on some shoes," she teased unsteadily. "I don't think there was any real danger. I...I just overreacted when I saw how they...how they..." She faltered, remembering the pathetically wilted leaves of the edelweiss, the shards of broken ceramic and glass.

"To hell with shoes." Daniel pulled her close again. "I told the police to meet me at your place. Do you want to wait here or come with me?"

Kerith sighed, allowing herself the luxury of his embrace for a moment, then pushing resolutely away. "I'd better come. Dressed as you are, you might be mistaken for the burglar," she joked weakly.

She couldn't, however, manage any humor when they surveyed the damage done to the rest of the house. Her bedroom looked ravaged, drawers pulled out, clothes and personal items strewn everywhere, the sheets on her bed stained with red wine taken from her own pantry.

"Looks like malicious mischief to me." The investigating officer looked up from the notes he'd been scribbling. "Are you sure you can't think of anyone who might do something like this? A disgruntled customer or maybe an ex-employee?"

Kerith's memory briefly flicked back to her confrontation with Arthur, then just as quickly discarded the idea. Arthur had been a model employee, since that night. He didn't deserve to be dragged into this just because he'd formed an unfortunate emotional attachment to his boss.

She shook her head firmly. "Sorry, there isn't anyone I can think of."

The policeman sighed. "Probably was kids, then. Occasionally we have some trouble with the ones whose parents work nights at the casinos. Judging by the money and jewelry you said were missing, and the clumsy way the back door was forced, I'd say it was youngsters too inexperienced or scared to try fencing any really big items."

"But why the destruction?" Kerith asked forlornly, picking up the remains of a favorite Hummel figurine.

The uniformed man shrugged. "I leave that to the psychiatrists. Do you have another place to stay tonight? Regardless of who did this, you shouldn't stay here until you get that door fixed. For that matter, I'd suggest you have a home-security system installed." He glanced meaningfully at her expensive television-and-stereo unit. "Next time, you might lose a lot more."

"Don't worry, I'll see that it's done," Daniel announced forcefully. He stepped forward to place a protective arm around Kerith's shoulders, then glanced down at her challengingly as he added, "In the meantime, she'll be staying with me."

8

"I STILL DON'T THINK this is a good idea." Kerith stubbornly folded her arms across her chest and faced Daniel from the doorway of his guest room. It had taken hours, handling the police, picking up the debris from the break-in and packing the things she would need for the night. Now, she was almost numb with fatigue, but she still felt the need to protest Daniel's plan.

He turned from placing her suitcase on a low chest and smiled patiently. "That's the twenty-fifth time you've said that, and you're still wrong. This is the perfect solution to your problem. You need a place to stay until your house is safe again, which could take several days, since we can't even call for an estimate on the security system until Monday. I not only have the room, I also like knowing you're safe, just in case that break-in was something more than a kid's prank." He crossed the room to her and pulled a small packet of folded papers from his pocket. "I found these before the police came and figured you'd prefer not having them read."

His notes! Those sexy, romantic missives she'd hidden in her jewelry box were as incriminating as evidence presented before a jury. "I . . . I was only . . ." she faltered, feeling a hot rush of embarrassment from her head to her toes.

"Shh." Daniel's fingertips pressed gently against her lips. "Don't try to explain. Let me dream a little."

At his touch, her flush deepened to a sensual heat that raced through her veins like liquid fire. She experienced a sweet, melting sensation deep within, reminding her of the part of him she carried there.

"I can't stay here," she said, even as her body swayed toward him. "Because I don't intend to go to bed with you again, and sooner or later that issue is going to come up."

Daniel took advantage of her movement toward him, pulling her close. "Hey, didn't I tell you I wouldn't push on that? Right now, I'm just happy to have you here. If anything more comes of it...well, that's up to you." He gave her a little squeeze and set her away from him. "All I want, for now, is the chance to take care of you."

Take care of you. At that moment, with the picture of her vandalized home still clear in her mind, no words could have sounded sweeter to Kerith. She accepted, adding quickly the situation was only temporary.

ALMOST BEFORE she knew it, temporary stretched into a week.

"The home-security business is booming right now," Daniel explained after he'd done some checking. "Installation dates are backlogged three weeks at the least."

Kerith promptly insisted she had to find another place to stay, but as the days passed she found herself settling into Daniel's home with unbelievable ease. After a while, she reluctantly admitted the reason to herself. She and Daniel suited each other.

Whereas she and Gus had coexisted, making allowances for the differences in their habits; her living patterns seemed to mesh with Daniel's like the hues of a fine watercolor. Even the occasionally unannounced visits of his relatives stopped bothering her after a while. Taken a few at a time, they weren't so bad, and she simply absented herself on the one occasion his mother appeared.

Her only lasting concern was over the inescapable current of desire that grew stronger between them with each passing day. She saw it in the flash of Daniel's dark eyes as he sat at breakfast, his fingers absently caressing the fuzzy leaves of her rescued edelweiss, which now held a place of honor on his breakfast bar. She felt it as a provocative ache deep in her abdomen each time she saw him arrive downstairs in the morning, freshly groomed, or lying rumpled and relaxed on the couch at the end of the day, listening to a favorite tape. She heard it in the affectionate way he teased her about his superior cooking skills as they shared the task of preparing dinner in his small kitchen. But most of all, she sensed it in the electric, waiting tension that hummed in the air whenever they occupied the same room. Strangely enough, an invitation to Thanksgiving dinner brought the waiting to an end.

DANIEL HESITANTLY brought the subject up after dinner one night, two days before the holiday. "My mother called today," he began, toying with the stem of his wineglass. "She told me I won't get any pumpkin pie if I don't talk you into having Thanksgiving dinner with the family."

"Think of the calories you'll save," Kerith teased, smiling to cover the sudden panic squeezing her stomach. But when she saw the disappointment clouding Daniel's eyes, she sobered. "You know how I feel about big family gatherings."

"It won't be like the birthday," he hastened to assure her. "Just my mom, my sisters and their families and us. No more than thirteen people, including you. You've gotten along with them whenever they came over here, how much more difficult can a small dinner be?"

Kerith got up quickly and started gathering dishes. "I can hardly believe your mother wants me there," she said offhandedly. "I saw the way she looked at me when you told her I was married to Gus. She probably thinks I'm after your money now."

"What the—" Daniel broke off in astonished laughter. "That's the most ridiculous thing I've ever heard. Ever since she met you, she's been driving me crazy asking when I was going to bring you again." He caught Kerith's hand and pulled her toward him. "She wants you to be a part of our holiday, almost as much as I do."

His simple pronouncement flowed like a healing balm over her anxious heart, and a new feeling unfurled there like a sun-warmed rosebud. "All...all right. I suppose I could come. But I can't promise to enjoy it."

"Thanks, love." Daniel smiled and raised her hand, and pressed his lips against the soft center of her palm.

It was the first time he'd kissed her since their current living arrangement had begun, and Kerith felt the warmth and softness of his mouth throughout every inch of her being. She shuddered, stepping back abruptly, and Daniel let out a soft groan.

"Sorry," he muttered after passing a hand roughly over his face. "I thought a simple hand kiss would be all right."

"It . . . it's okay," Kerith stammered, busying herself with clearing the table. "You've been very good about keeping your word." Which made it totally unreasonable for her to wish he had less fortitude, she told herself sharply as she headed for the kitchen. But she did wish it. And she was more than a little disappointed when he made no further move toward her. After the dishes were done, he excused himself to go work out in the small gym contained within the condominium complex.

"Sister Agnes always said you were perverse," Kerith grumbled to herself as she prepared for bed a while later. "Always wanting what you couldn't have." Except, she could have Daniel—if she was willing to accept the emotional entanglements that came with him. The real obstacle was her lingering fear of those entanglements.

Still muttering to herself, she scurried down the hall to the bathroom for a glass of water. Her last ritual each night was taking one of the prenatal vitamins the doctor had prescribed. Not bothering to turn on the light, she quickly filled a glass and swallowed the large pink pill. She nearly dropped the glass, however, when the connecting door to the master bedroom swung open and the light came on to reveal Daniel standing there in nearly naked splendor.

Equally startled, they exclaimed almost in unison.

"Oh! I thought you were . . ."

"Sorry, I thought you were . . ."

Kerith smiled weakly and finished, "working out" as her eyes skittered nervously away from the towel fastened precariously low on his hips. His hair was slicked back, still damp from the shower, and there were a few diamond-bright droplets caught in the light furring on his chest.

She saw Daniel's biceps bulge slightly as he gripped the doorjamb and let his gaze travel slowly down the flower-sprigged length of her sheer cotton nightgown. When he brought his eyes up again, they rested for a breath-catching moment on the soft swell of her breasts not covered by the scooped neckline. He inhaled sharply and stared at the floor, the muscles in his arms tightening even more.

"I swear, Kerith, you are the most beautiful woman I've ever seen," he said in a low, anguished voice. "Having you here and not being able to touch you is the sweetest torture I've ever known."

Sweet torture. Yes, that's what it is, Kerith thought, her body pulsing with sensual excitement. And what had she gained denying it, except frustration and loneliness? Were those any better than the potential pain of being vulnerable again? "Daniel, I . . ." She faltered, overwhelmed by the magnitude of the decision she was making.

"No, you don't have to repeat all the reasons you can't," he said, misinterpreting her hesitation. "I made a promise, and I'll keep it." He looked up, disappointment plain in his rueful smile. "But if you ever change your mind, I'll make sure you don't regret it." He stepped back into his bedroom, preparing to shut the door, but Kerith's voice rang out, stopping him cold.

"Is that a promise?" For a moment, she was surprised she'd actually spoken, but then she felt only certainty.

"You can count on it, love." A very different smile curved Daniel's attractive mouth as he watched her walk toward him. When their bodies were almost touching, she reached up and stroked one hand down the powerful curve of his chest, over the taut, smooth skin covering his ribs and further, until she was touching his flat, hard belly just above the knot of the towel. His breath sucked in, and the silky hair on his groin tickled her palm.

Daniel's eyes searched hers with a newborn urgency. "Will you consider me barbaric if I haul you right off to my bed? Because I'm almost at the end of my endurance. Even the workouts aren't helping anymore."

Laughing softly, Kerith shook her head, then let out a soft shriek when he immediately swung her up in his arms and proceeded to do as he'd threatened. The sheets of his neatly turned-down bed were cool against her back when he laid her on it, but his skin was hot beneath her fingertips as he stretched out beside her. His mouth came down on hers with the hunger of a man too long denied, and Kerith returned the kiss with all her own pent-up desire. They writhed and twisted, arms and legs tangling until Kerith's hand encountered the knot of Daniel's towel. After only an instant of hesitation, she tugged it loose, and the rigid heat of his erection filled her hand. With a soft murmur of appreciation, she stroked the satiny skin stretched taut over his iron-hard shaft...relearning...adoring... Too soon, he pulled away, gasping.

"Not so fast, love," he growled softly. "I have a few other things in mind first." His mouth sought the silken curve of her throat as he gently eased the wide neckline of her nightgown down. But she had to stifle a cry, when his strong hands molded her breasts.

Daniel's concern was instantaneous. "What is it, sweetheart? Was I too rough?"

Kerith froze. She couldn't tell him pregnancy was the cause of that unusual tenderness. "I . . . I'm just a little sensitive there sometimes. It's fine now."

"It doesn't hurt if I do this?" His fingers moved ever so gently, their skill tantalizing beyond belief. "Or this?" His mouth formed a soft, moist prison around her puckered nipple.

Kerith gasped in helpless pleasure. "That . . . that's wonderful. Please . . . please don't stop." And he didn't, although he drove her half mad with gentleness. She felt her nightgown being slipped off, felt his gentle hands and avid mouth tasting, praising, worshiping her body like a celebrant at a shrine. She was quivering and damp with need by the time he paused to take care of protecting her, and she nearly cried out in frustration that it wasn't necessary. But then he was back, surging heavily into the satiny tightness of her body, driving her to a shuddering explosion almost immediately. Kerith grabbed frantically for the solid strength of Daniel's shoulders, as pleasure rocked through her in waves. She was only vaguely aware when his arms gave out and he collapsed on her with a guttural cry of release.

A long while passed before Daniel found the strength to roll over onto his back, bringing Kerith's limp form with him. Never had he felt more drained or exhausted. And yet, within his innermost being there was a surging joy, a singing elation that paradoxically made him want to weep. How perfect lovemaking could be when the love was real—and what a travesty without it. If only he could tell Kerith all that was in his heart…

He brought himself up short. No, not yet. The specter of Edelweiss remained between them. Damn Lucretia! The last time he'd called in she'd been as vague as ever, regarding any kind of time schedule. And when he'd told her about the break-in and his new living arrangement, she'd been positively obnoxious.

"I knew you still had it, Casanova. There isn't a woman alive who could resist sleeping with you," she'd crowed triumphantly.

"I didn't say she was sleeping with me," he'd responded coldly. "I brought her here for protection."

Lucretia sobered temporarily. "Does that mean you think the break-in night not be simple vandalism? If there's any hint of trouble, I want to know."

"Don't worry about it. I checked things out before the police arrived. The place was vandalized, but it wasn't searched, not by anyone who knew what he was doing, anyway. It looked like the work of juvenile delinquents, to me."

"Keep your eyes open, regardless. And stick as close to the lady as possible. I have a hunch we'll be hearing from our foreign friends soon."

Soon being a relative term, Daniel amended, coming back to the present at a soft, contented sound from Kerith. It reminded him of the purr of a cat. *She* reminded him of a cat, with that sleek, golden body of hers and those sexy, up-tilted eyes. Did she understand how vital she was to his happiness? At least he could tell her that, even if the love part had to wait. "Are you asleep?" he asked quietly when she shifted in his arms.

"Mmm, no. But I'm not too sure I'm still alive. I feel like the victim of a cyclone."

Daniel chuckled softly and brushed the silky, golden tangle of hair back from her face. "I know what you mean. But I also feel more alive than I ever have before. You do that, Kerith. And it makes me want to hold on to you forever." He felt the caution tighten her body, even before she spoke.

"Daniel, I think you should understand something. What just happened, it doesn't come with any guarantees. I can't promise you forever, or even next week." She raised her head from his chest and looked at him, uncertainty creasing her brow.

"Then we'll take it one day at a time. I can be very patient when I try," he assured her, gently stroking the tension from her forehead. "Just allow me the chance to sway your thinking." He pulled her closer and teased the swollen softness of her mouth with a flick of his tongue.

"I should warn you, however," he added with a grin. "I can be very convincing."

Slowly, deliberately, she ran her tongue over her top lip, savoring the lingering taste of his kisses. "That sounds like a threat. What devious means do you plan to employ?"

"How about a little old-fashioned domination?" With a lunge, he turned over, pinning her beneath his hard body.

Kerith merely laughed and lightly trailed her fingernails over the sensitive hollow at the base of his spine. Daniel arched his back and let out a low, guttural sound. Almost at once, she felt a burgeoning hardness begin to press against her inner thigh.

"For a late bloomer, you certainly picked this up fast," Daniel accused, his dark eyes glinting with renewed fire.

Kerith laughed again and flexed her fingers against his tautly muscled buttocks. "I've always been a quick study."

"That may be, but I can make love in five languages." He gave her a teasing leer, then sealed her mouth with a deep, hungry kiss.

"I'm fluent in six," she gasped when he'd finished.

"Ah, but can you make love in them?" His mouth trailed down to her jaw and he nibbled her chin lightly.

She tried to answer, but could only manage a moan as he slid down to give loving attention to her breasts.

"Que magnifique!" he murmured. The velvet roughness of his tongue rubbed over her contracted nipple, and she began to quiver with the inner hunger only he could satisfy.

He moved lower and kissed the tender hollow beside her hipbone, then inched lower still. *"Je t'adore"*, he whispered over the gentle mound of her womanhood. And then she felt his tongue caress her with a breathtaking intimacy that brought shimmering star bursts of release.

"Je t'adore," she echoed impulsively, urging him up until she felt the heavy pressure of his manhood seeking entry. And then he was surging into her, swift and

deep, and her world shattered into bright prisms of sheer pleasure.

They didn't make it past French that night.

KERITH AWAKENED on Thanksgiving day with strong misgivings about her coming encounter with the Avanti family. But making slow, exquisite love with Daniel helped a lot. In fact, making love had become a panacea for a lot of her doubts.

Maybe that had something to do with why they did it so often, she mused, as she settled back in the Firebird's passenger seat. Daniel had taken the wheel for the drive to his mother's house, and she found it reassuring to watch his strong, competent hands guiding the powerful car. Just as they had guided her body, again and again . . .

She cut off the thought, faint color touching her cheeks. That certainly wasn't the kind of thing to think of now. Not when faced with the ordeal of interacting with the man's family.

"What are you thinking about?" Daniel braked for a traffic signal and glanced at her with eyes still glowing from the morning's activities.

"Nothing."

"Oh, yes, you are. I can see it in your eyes." He grinned and turned his attention back to the road as the light changed. "And if you keep looking at me like that, my mother is going to start asking me if my intentions are honorable."

Kerith flinched a little, remembering one of her main worries. "Does . . . does she know I'm staying with you?"

"Yes." Daniel caught her anxious expression and hastened to assure her. "I told her what happened to your house, and she said I did the right thing, moving you to my place." He gave her a teasing grin. "She might be harboring secret hopes, though. Mothers tend to be that way when they have unmarried sons my age."

Panic leapt anew in Kerith's heart. "Daniel, I don't think I can do this. What if she asks me if my intentions are honorable?"

Gentle laughter rumbled deep in Daniel's chest, and he reached to give her hand a comforting squeeze. "She wouldn't do that. My mother may be old-fashioned about some things, but she also has class. Stop worrying, love. Everything is going to be fine."

To her surprise, he was right. After a few awkward moments when they first arrived, the warmth and gaiety of Daniel's relatives swept over Kerith, drawing her in. Added to that were the rich, inviting aromas of roasting turkey and freshly baked pies. It soon became evident Rosa Avanti's only concession to old-fashioned ideas was an overloaded table.

In fact, the only uncomfortable moment came when Daniel chose to announce with a devilish twinkle in his eyes, that Kerith was quite fluent in Italian. Remembering how he had tested her fluency that morning in bed, Kerith nearly choked on a bite of pumpkin pie. Luckily, no one seemed to notice, and Rosa quickly drew Kerith into a lively discussion of Italy. Since Kerith had visited that country several times, talking about it was easy, and from there the day only got better.

LATER THAT NIGHT, as she lay cuddled with Daniel, pleasantly exhausted from yet another test of their linguistic skills, Kerith was struck again by how easy it all had seemed. Was it possible she'd been fooling herself all these years, thinking she was better off living without any emotional commitment? And the unborn child she carried, was it fair to deprive it of such a warm, loving family as the Avantis?

One way or another, she would have to make a decision soon. Her waistline was beginning to thicken, and Daniel was sure to notice before long. If she intended to stay with him, she would have to tell him about the child. The thought of how little time she had, made her squirm restlessly. At once, she felt Daniel's arms tighten protectively around her waist, and the instant comfort that unconscious gesture brought, made her wonder if the decision had been made already. As she drifted off to a troubled sleep, she resolved to talk it over with Ali as soon as possible.

But when Ali arrived at work on Monday morning, she had some unsettling news of her own.

"Congratulate me, I'm getting married!"

"What?" Kerith turned from the spectacular sunrise outside her office window and gaped at her radiantly smiling friend.

"I said, I'm getting married. Sam proposed over the weekend, and I accepted."

Kerith tried to hide her dismay. "Isn't this a little sudden?" she asked faintly.

Ali shrugged and joined her at the window. "Not really. We've been neighbors for ages." She grinned and toasted herself with the coffee cup she carried. "And he says he's been in love with me almost since the day he moved in next door. He was just waiting for me to settle down and notice."

Sunlight poured through the window, warming Kerith's back, but inside she felt a chill of uncertainty. So many changes had taken place in her life lately. When Ali married, their friendship would change, too, including the amount of time they spent together.

But you have Daniel now, an inner voice reminded her. *Or you could, if you'd stop hesitating.*

"Hey, in there." Ali waved a slender hand in front of Kerith's eyes. "You don't look very happy for me. I thought you liked Sam."

Kerith summoned a bright smile. "Of course I'm happy. And Sam's a wonderful man. Your news just took me by surprise." She took Ali's arm and urged her toward the couch. "Sit down and tell me your plans. I hope this doesn't mean you'll be leaving Classique. I can't say I'll be overjoyed at that prospect."

Ali laughed. "Don't worry, I'm not quitting unless I get really crazy and decide to have another baby." She glanced meaningfully at Kerith's middle. "Speaking of which, have you told Daniel yet? You're bound to start showing before too much longer."

"I'm still wearing my regular clothes," Kerith protested, one hand going self-consciously to her stomach. "The doctor said I could go another month like this." He'd also jokingly assured her that an active sex life wouldn't harm the baby as long as she didn't go in for chains and whips. Kerith grinned, remembering.

"How can you look so happy, while you're still deceiving that poor man?" Ali sighed irritably. "I've never seen you look more . . . I don't know . . . content."

Unsettled by Ali's perception, Kerith rose quickly and walked to her desk before speaking. "Actually, I am more content lately. And I've even considered telling Daniel about the child." Her mouth twisted in wry humor. "Unfortunately, I can't seem to come up with the right way to do it after holding back so long."

"Don't worry about the method, just do it," Ali urged, coming over to perch on the corner of the desk. "The man's so crazy in love with you, he'd forgive almost anything."

"Perhaps he would, but that doesn't help me with the other consequences of telling him." Kerith sat down in her executive chair and restlessly ran her hands down the smooth, leather arms. "He's a family-oriented man. And I'm still not sure I can handle a commitment like that."

"You've been living with the guy for weeks."

"That's a long way from marriage."

Ali slapped her hands down to her thighs in exasperation. "Okay, I can't tell you what to do with your life, but I do feel compelled to say this—Daniel Avanti is one fantastic man and, believe me, they are few and far between in this world. You'd better think carefully before you reject what he's offering. Speech ended." Ali stood up, straightened the razor-sharp crease in her uniform trousers, and walked to the door. "I have to go—early pickup today. But think about what I said."

Kerith smiled ruefully. "Rest assured, I'll probably think of little else until this is resolved. And by the way, I wish you and Sam and Cami all the best."

Ali smiled over her shoulder. "Thanks. I'm wishing that for you and Daniel, too."

If only wishes were enough, Kerith thought, picking up a sheaf of letters requiring signatures. Yet, deep inside she agreed with Ali. Daniel was a fantastic man.

For the rest of the day Kerith mulled it over, weighing pros and cons until her head spun. By the time she was ready to leave that evening, however, she'd talked herself into telling Daniel of his prospective fatherhood. With a determined step she headed for the door, but then the intercom buzzed, calling her back.

"There's a woman on line one who wants to speak to you, but she refuses to give her name," Charlotte explained apologetically. "She sounds kind of foreign— claims it's extremely important."

Kerith sighed, glancing at her watch. She'd probably be late getting home to Daniel, but being in business required catering to the eccentricities of a potential client. "I'll take the call. Who knows? It could be Marlene Dietrich or the Queen of England." Charlotte chuckled sympathetically and put the call through.

After politely announcing herself, Kerith waited, but the only response she got was the sound of a softly indrawn breath and then the hollow hum of an open line.

She tried again, with a little more force. "This is Kerith Anders. Who's calling, please?"

"I . . . I'm sorry." The woman's voice, although hesitant, had a melodious precision that demanded attention. "My name is Julia Robbins. We haven't met, but I know you, Kerith. I've known you for a long time."

A little frisson of apprehension ran down Kerith's spine, but she made herself respond calmly. "Your name isn't familiar to me. Have we done business before?"

"No, never." The woman made a sharp, frustrated sound. "I knew this would be difficult. Perhaps I should just state it plainly. I . . . I'm your mother. And I would like very much to meet you."

Kerith's first reaction was stunned disbelief. "Is this some kind of joke? I don't have a mother."

A deep sigh came from the other end of the line. "No, no joke. When we meet you'll see . . ."

"Why should I agree to meet you?" Kerith demanded, a sick premonition stirring to life in her stomach. "I have no way of knowing what you're saying is true. Can you prove it?"

"Quite easily." There was a brief pause, and then the cultured voice announced quietly, "I am Edelweiss."

9

IRREPRESSIBLE OPTIMISM put a spring in Daniel's step as he entered Kerith's office, a fragrant bouquet of mixed flowers in one hand. But his step faltered and his smile of anticipation faded when he found her sitting hunched over at her desk, arms clasped around her middle, features pale and stricken.

He rushed to her side, the flowers falling to the floor, forgotten. "Kerith, honey, what is it? Are you ill?"

She looked at him as if she hadn't even noticed his arrival until that moment. "Edelweiss," she murmured vaguely.

Daniel was instantly alert. "What about Edelweiss? Come on, Kerith, talk to me." He gave her a little shake which seemed to bring her back to her senses.

"I'm sorry, I guess the phone call gave me a bit of a shock."

"What phone call?" Daniel demanded sharply. But he knew, even before she spoke, and frustration swept over him in a boiling tide. Why now? After all the months of unexplained delay, why did it have to come just when he'd begun to make real progress with her?

"Edelweiss called me." Kerith laughed shakily. "Now, doesn't that sound like the shocker of the year? But it isn't. The real news is, I have a mother. I never was an orphan."

Daniel sat back on his heels in surprise, his hands falling from her shoulders. "Edelweiss told you that you have a mother?"

Kerith laughed again, a faint hysteria echoing in the mirthless sound. "Edelweiss *is* my mother," she announced, jumping up to pace over to one window and back. "Can you believe that?" she asked, eyes widening incredulously. "I never even thought of Edelweiss as a woman."

Daniel stood to face her. "Why not? Flower names are generally considered feminine."

"But what kind of woman would treat her child as she treated me?" Kerith threw out her hands in exasperation. "She abandoned me!"

"Perhaps she had her reasons," Daniel suggested, thinking of Lucretia's allusions to Edelweiss's elevated rank. It could explain a lot. He'd heard a few horror stories about retaliation against the friends and relatives of top-level agents.

"I don't give a damn about her reasons," Kerith said coldly. "I told her I didn't want to meet her."

Dread settled like a millstone in Daniel's chest. At this point he didn't really care about his agreement to aid Edelweiss in arranging the meeting. What did distress him was the sudden detachment he saw in Kerith's eyes when she looked at him. The barriers were going up again, stronger than ever, and he sensed there might be only one irreversible way to do away with them— through Edelweiss.

Shoving his hands into the pockets of his slacks, he said carefully, "Don't you think you owe it to yourself to at least get a few answers before you tell her to get lost? I got the impression you've always wanted to know about your heritage." Her belligerent scowl wavered a bit, and he knew he'd scored a hit.

"What can it hurt to let the woman tell her story? No one can force you to change the way you feel." Silently, he sent up a fervent prayer that Edelweiss could, indeed, do just that.

"I don't know . . ." Kerith was shaking her head, but she looked uncertain. "I probably won't like what she has to say."

Daniel reached out and gave her shoulders an encouraging little squeeze. "You won't know that until you hear it."

Kerith looked up at him, apprehension unexpectedly adding an endearing childishness to her lovely face. "I don't think I could face her alone. What would I say to her?"

"I'll be there if you like. In fact, if it makes you feel better, you can ask her to come over to my place. That way, you'll have the advantage of familiar surroundings." *And Edelweiss will have her damned security. Very smooth, Casanova*, an inner voice mocked. His earlier dread became an oppressive weight. How the hell was he going to explain his role in all this to her?

The answer was, he couldn't. Not yet, anyway. Kerith didn't need that kind of news right now. He could only hope the meeting with Edelweiss wouldn't make matters worse.

"I suppose it wouldn't be too bad, as long as she doesn't expect anything of me," Kerith said reluctantly.

Hope welled up, easing a little the load on Daniel's heart. "You're a grown woman now. She can't control you as she did when you were a child."

A grim little smile tugged at Kerith's lovely mouth. "You're right. She said she'd call again tomorrow, just in case I'd changed my mind. I'll just tell her we're dealing on my terms now."

"Good for you." Daniel gave her a smile of encouragement, but he worried over the cool determination he saw in her eyes.

IT WAS STILL there the next evening, as they waited for the arrival of Kerith's mother. When the doorbell rang, however, Kerith turned to him in sudden panic.

"I'll get it," he offered, rising quickly from the couch.

He opened the front door, prepared to offer a cordial welcome, but the smile froze half formed at the sight waiting for him outside. It was like being zapped through a time tunnel into the future, he thought vaguely, as he stared in shock at the woman before him. Except for the deep blue eyes, and the delicate ivory skin tone, she looked exactly as he imagined Kerith would look twenty, maybe thirty years from now.

"Hello, Mr. . . . Avanti, isn't it?" she inquired, shifting the ornate cane she held to her left hand so she could offer the right one in greeting. "I'm Julia Robbins." She glanced over her shoulder at a craggy-featured man who stood behind her on the stoop. "This is my. . . friend Karl Barber."

Daniel wasn't fooled by the man's iron-gray hair and neat business suit. The guy was an agent. Extra protection, maybe? Yet, when the introductions were complete and Daniel invited them inside, he could have sworn he heard the man mutter, "Careful of the step, honey," as Julia limped forward.

Kerith heard their footsteps in the hallway, and jumped up off the couch to take a position by the fireplace. The cheerful blaze Daniel had built earlier did nothing for the chill in her hands, but standing gave her confidence a boost. Straightening her spine, she prepared herself for whatever was to come, then stiffened in surprise when Daniel and two strangers appeared in the arched doorway to the living room.

No, both weren't exactly strangers. There was something vaguely familiar about the woman, Kerith thought, as random impressions avalanched her mind: chic, black suit, rose silk blouse, shiny hair curving forward to frame a slightly exotic face.

What was it about that face . . . ? The truth, when it hit her was an unwelcome shock. *I look like her,* Kerith realized, stricken. She'd been prepared to hate an anonymous stranger; it was another matter, to scorn a face as familiar as her own.

"Kerith, this is Julia Robbins and her . . . friend Karl Barber," Daniel said smoothly, breaking the awkward silence.

Then the woman moved forward and Kerith received another unpleasant surprise. The confident bearing and slim, supple body were marred by a painful limp. "Hello, Kerith," the woman said, her voice bearing the rich accent associated with England's upper class. "I've been looking forward to this day for a long time." She made a move as if to offer her hand, and Kerith almost recoiled.

"Please come in, have a seat...uh, Ms Robbins," she said quickly, wanting to avoid any physical contact.

The smile she got in response was rueful. "Thank you, but I'd rather stand, if you don't mind. We've been traveling for quite a while, and sitting is a little uncomfortable at the moment." She waved a graceful hand toward the couch. "You needn't stand, though. And please call me Julia. Heaven knows, the situation is awkward enough without unnecessary formality."

The men moved first to comply, and Karl stopped next to Julia long enough to lay a gentle hand on the silky hair curving against her nape before taking a seat at the far end of the couch. Daniel settled on the section that extended toward the fireplace on the opposite end. After a moment's hesitation, Kerith perched in the center of the long expanse of cushions between the two men.

Uneasy silence settled over the room as Julia slowly made her way to stand before them, a heavy stillness like that of an audience waiting for the opening curtain of an anxiously awaited play. It seemed to rob Julia of some of her poise, and she turned uncertainly to Karl. "Now that I'm here, I'm not sure how to begin."

Karl sat forward, his rather harsh features softening briefly in a smile. When he spoke, Kerith detected a slight Texas accent. "Just start at the beginning, and tell it all straight through. I'm sure Mrs. Anders will let you know, if she has questions."

Kerith assented with a quick nod, and Julia began. "Have you heard of an organization called Interpol?"

At the back of Kerith's mind, a little warning light clicked on. "Of course. It's sort of an international law-enforcement agency, isn't it?"

Julia nodded. "I've been one of their agents since I was twenty-one."

An agent! Kerith barely suppressed a startled guffaw. What was this, some kind of weird joke? She threw Daniel a questioning glance, and the look he sent back unsettled her more. Why did he suddenly look as if he'd been convicted of a crime? Something didn't feel right here . . . She left the thought half formed as Julia went on.

"I can see you're having difficulty assimilating this, and I don't blame you. My career and my life have been a bit out of the ordinary. Perhaps I should explain how it began. You see, I was quite alone in the world when I was approached. My parents had died of influenza two years previously, and I had no other living relatives. I'd just left university, wasn't sure what I'd do next. The people who recruited me offered job security and what sounded like an enormous amount of money." Julia's mouth twisted in a wry smile. "More than that, they convinced me I could actually make a contribution to world peace, and I was quite an idealist at the time."

"You *have* made significant contributions," Karl put in gruffly, but Julia silenced him with a gentle shake of her head.

"My first assignment was in Germany, and I met and fell in love with your father there."

"Was he an agent, also?" Kerith asked, remembering the times in her childhood when she'd toyed with that particular daydream—especially after seeing one of the more glamorized spy movies.

"He was a courier for the British government. Although, by nationality, he was Greek." Julia dropped her eyes for a moment, and when she looked up again there was a haunting sadness in them. "You inherited your coloring from him. Your eyes..." She appeared to sag a little, and when she turned to take a step, she stumbled.

Karl was beside her in an instant. "Perhaps you'd better sit for a while, hon—" He cut off the endearment too late.

Julia resisted briefly, then gave in and let him lead her to a place near Kerith on the couch. "Your father's name was Jon," she continued, when she was settled. "I think I loved him from the first instant I saw him. It was like being struck by lightning."

Kerith felt a vicarious tug. Hadn't she experienced something similar with Daniel? But that couldn't have been love... Shaking off the thought, she quickly asked, "What happened to him?"

Julia lowered her gaze to her tightly clenched hands. "He . . . he was killed. I discovered later it was something to do with the East Germans. I . . . I found out I was pregnant two days afterward, so he never knew about you. If he had, I suppose we would have married. We'd discussed it, but as long as we were under assignment, it wasn't possible. He talked often about how it would be when we were both free. He called it our golden future. When he died, I felt as if my future had gone with him. All I had left was the past, the present and my work."

"And me," Kerith put in shortly. Up to that point, she'd been listening with a stunned detachment, but now the story began to take on a painful reality.

Julia nodded, her tawny hair swinging forward to brush her jawline. "Yes, there was you. When I told my superiors I was pregnant, they were furious. Relationships are strictly forbidden when you're in the field. They wanted me to have an abortion, but I refused. The thought of having a child terrified me, but you were the only part of Jon I had left, and I couldn't bring myself to destroy that."

"Then why did you give me away?" Kerith demanded, her voice tight with the betrayal that had haunted her for years.

"Because I believed it was my only option." Julia looked up, her blue eyes beseeching. "Please, try to understand. At the time I was torn with grief over Jon. I didn't know if I could take care of myself, let alone an infant. When my employer offered to keep me on, with the prevision that I give you up, I didn't have the will to refuse. My work seemed to be the only secure thing in my life just then."

Without warning, Kerith's tightly reined emotions broke free. "Then why didn't you really let me go?" she demanded, her voice raw. "Why didn't you release me for adoption?"

Julia flinched, and the delicate color of her face faded to stark white. "Because, you were all I had left of my future. In the hospital, when they came to take you away, I realized I couldn't let go completely. I had this dream of one day finding a way for us to be together. So I devised an interim plan for your care and education." She shook her head remorsefully. "By the time I admitted to myself the improbability of my dream, it was too late. You were long past the age when adoption is likely."

With a harsh sound, Kerith jumped up and stalked to the fireplace where she grabbed a poker and began jabbing viciously at a sputtering log. "Did you ever think of my dreams? Did you ever consider what it felt like, not knowing who I was or where I belonged? You say you provided for me, but you never gave me the one thing I really needed—a sense of belonging." Damn, how could she still feel the hurt so intensely?

Unable to hold back anymore, she let it all out. "You had it all your way, didn't you? Making sure I was always tied to you, yet protecting yourself from any emotional commitment by hiding behind your damned shield of secrecy."

"Now, hold on," Karl interjected, rising quickly from his seat to stand between the two women. He gave Julia an apologetic glance. "I know I agreed not to interfere, but someone has to state a few facts here." He turned on Kerith, his gray eyes fierce. "Your mother left out a few important details. First, she is one of the most important agents in our organization. Her gift for languages and her extraordinary memory are invaluable in our line of work. Which is why our people were so anxious to have her back after your birth. You can believe they did everything in their power to convince her to give you up. Second, being that important comes with a high price."

"Karl, please," Julia protested, looking pained. "It isn't going to make any difference."

"Maybe not, but I'm going to say it anyway." He glared at Kerith. "You think of her secrecy as an act of cruelty, but did you ever consider that it might have been meant to protect you? Your mother and I are in a dangerous business; sometimes we make enemies who aren't above taking their revenge out on the innocent."

His implication hit Kerith like a cold dash of water. She moved away from him until against her back she felt the cool, rough texture of the white bricks surrounding the fireplace. Edelweiss a protector? No, impossible! The concept challenged too many lifelong convictions. Yet, when she looked again at Julia, she experienced a whisper of uncertainty.

"Yes, look at her," Karl continued forcefully. "She's still recovering from the injuries she sustained on her last assignment. She shouldn't even be here."

"Then, why did you come?" Kerith asked Julia in a low, anguished voice. "Why now?"

Julia sighed, and absentmindedly rubbed a hand down the length of her injured thigh. "Because I've been forced to retire. And to do that, I must undergo a complete change of identity—including plastic surgery." She opened her eyes and gave Kerith a poignant smile. "I wanted you to see the resemblance between us before it's forever erased. And I wanted to tell you, just once, that I loved you."

Kerith reared back like someone dodging a blow. Being asked to acknowledge the extenuating circumstances behind Julia's actions was one thing, but accepting belated declarations of love was quite another. Eyes narrowed accusingly she said, "If you had really loved me, you wouldn't have been able to give me up in the first place."

Like a lion defending its mate, Karl turned on her. "Who are you to judge her? Can you be so sure you wouldn't make the same decisions if you and that kid you're carrying were in the same situation?"

Shocked silence followed his harsh inquiry, broken only by the dry snap and crackle of the fire. Then Daniel's voice came quietly. "What kid?"

Kerith scarcely heard him over the roaring storm of outrage sweeping her senses. "How did you know about that?" she demanded angrily. "Did this . . . this reunion require that you pry into my personal life?" The look Karl exchanged with Julia was answer enough. "I don't believe this. You actually had me investigated." Remembering her wrecked home, she grew even angrier. "I suppose it was necessary to ransack my home too, right?"

Karl looked confused. "Ransacked? What's she talking about?"

"A completely unrelated incident," Daniel supplied impatiently. "Damn it, Kerith, are you pregnant?"

Even in the midst of her turmoil, Kerith experienced a flash of guilt. Of all the rotten ways to have it come out . . . But before she could offer an explanation, Julia spoke up.

"You didn't know? We'd assumed you were being kept informed."

The urge to explain vanished, as a darker suspicion introduced itself. Daniel informed? But that would mean he was involved in this, too . . . One look at his face made it all disastrously clear. Of course, he was involved. He'd told her himself he was an agent—one who specialized in seducing women. What an utter fool she'd been, believing that story about his retirement, letting him get past her defenses until she had actually begun to care for him. When all along she'd been just another assignment to him, another victim of his infamous charm. The idea sickened her.

"Kerith, don't look at me like that," Daniel said, beginning to rise. "You don't understand."

"Oh, yes I do. I understand perfectly, now." Pressing one hand to her churning stomach, she started toward the door, but as she passed the couch, Julia waylaid her with an outstretched hand.

"You mustn't blame Daniel. He was brought into this for your protection. I couldn't take any chances, where your safety was concerned."

"Protection?" Kerith laughed scornfully. "He hardly qualifies for that job. He's the reason I'm pregnant."

Julia's mouth dropped open in surprise, and Karl made a rough sound of astonishment.

Apparently I wasn't the only one being kept in the dark, Kerith thought with some satisfaction. That knowledge alone seemed to restore some of her self-possession.

"You'll have to excuse me now," she said coldly, starting for the door again. "I've had enough lies and deception to last a lifetime." At the arched doorway, she paused and turned back for a final word. "I'm sure you'll be able to entertain yourselves without me. You can exchange techniques for manipulating people."

She heard them calling her name, as she ran up the stairs, but she didn't hesitate. She needed to get away, as far away as possible. But before she could do that, she had to find her purse and keys.

"IS THIS WHAT you're looking for?" Daniel inquired a few minutes later. He stood in the doorway to his bedroom, her small shoulder bag clutched in one hand.

"Yes, thank you." She stepped out of the closet and started toward him, then stopped short when he moved into the room and closed the door behind him. "I'm leaving," she announced decisively.

"Not until you let me explain." He looked implacable.

"I've had too many explanations already." She walked toward him, her hand outstretched. "The purse, please."

He simply hid it behind his back. "You'll have to listen, first. I can imagine what you're thinking, and you're not leaving until you hear the truth. I hated lying to you. I wouldn't have accepted this assignment if there had been any other way. I'm not Casanova, not anymore."

"Why should I believe that?" Kerith arched one brow skeptically. "It sounds to me as if I'm just another of Casanova's ladies. One of the gullible multitude who've been seduced by your charm."

"No!" Daniel dropped her purse and grabbed her shoulders roughly. "It wasn't like that with you, and you know it!"

"Do I?" She tipped her head back and glared at him. "You're just like those two downstairs. Living lies, telling half truths whenever it suits your purpose."

Daniel's dark eyes narrowed accusingly. "And what about you? Haven't you been doing the same? How do you think it felt, having a total stranger tell me the woman I love is carrying my child?"

The woman he loved. A small tremor ran through Kerith's heart, but it had no chance against her over-riding sense of betrayal. "Don't talk to me about love," she snapped. "You and that woman down in your living room don't even know the meaning of the word."

"That's where you're wrong," Daniel countered. When she tried to twist away, he tightened his grip and herded her backward until she sat down on the bed with a bounce. "I concealed my involvement with Edelweiss, but I never lied to you about my feelings. On the other hand, I don't think you've been exactly honest with yourself in that area." He grabbed the valet chair standing near the closet and seated himself on it before her. As he gazed at her, his expression softened.

"I do love you, Kerith. I would have told you long before now, but I had to wait until there could be complete honesty between us."

Again Kerith felt a fluttering in her heart, only this time it was stronger. Unwilling to give in to it, she forced her attention to the deep blue velvet of the bedspread. But as her hand moved restively over the soft, thick nap, she had an unexpected memory of how it had felt against her naked skin as Daniel made slow, delicious love to her. No! Not love, lust. And yet, she found herself hesitating at the thought of simply storming out of his life. In the midst of her anger, a small voice tempted her to believe him.

Her hand clenched convulsively around a wad of the rich fabric. "I'd be a fool to believe you."

Daniel reached out and touched her cheek. "Kerith, look at me." When she complied, he smiled sympathetically. "I know you've had a lot thrown at you this evening. But I want you to stop a minute and think of how it's been between us for the last few weeks. I've never loved any other woman as I love you. And I'd begun to hope you might feel the same way some day. I want to share my life with you—" Deliberately, he lowered his eyes to her stomach, then looked up again. "—and our baby. But I don't think that's possible until you stop letting the past rule your life."

Again, Kerith experienced a small quake of uncertainty. Could he be right? She shook her head and looked away. "You don't know what you're asking."

"Don't I? From the first time you told me about Edelweiss, I knew this meeting wouldn't be easy. But I allowed myself to hope it would help you ultimately. I don't condone what your mother did, but I do think you should forgive her, for your own sake."

She turned toward him, her chin tilting defensively, a stubborn denial on her tongue, but when their eyes met the certainty of his love crashed over her like a tidal wave. And with it came a more fundamental knowledge—she had fallen in love with him. The feeling flooded her heart, overwhelming indignation and damaged pride. It also unnerved her completely.

"I...I can't think here," she exclaimed, springing off the bed like a frightened rabbit. "I need to get away for a while."

"Kerith, wait," Daniel called, rising to follow as she hurried toward the door. "You can't drive when you're upset like this; it isn't safe."

"Then I'll walk."

"It's dark outside. I don't like the idea of you being out there alone."

Impatiently she shrugged off his concern. "I did a pretty good job taking care of myself before you came along. Don't push me right now, Daniel. You might not like the outcome."

"All right," he agreed reluctantly. "But only if you promise not to go far."

"Whatever you say." Quiet and solitude, that's what she needed to sort this all out.

"And don't stay out too long," he added, as she dashed down the stairs and out the front door.

The night air had an invigorating chill that made Kerith grateful for the long sleeves of the white sweater dress she'd chosen for the meeting with Julia Robbins. Overhead a pearlescent slice of moon adorned the night sky, but offered little illumination. Remembering her promise, she decided to confine her walk to the landscaped inner courtyard shared by Daniel and his neighbors.

A brisk wind swished eerily through the branches of palm trees and huge hibiscus bushes as she strolled by them. She shivered, her mind straying to the firelit warmth of Daniel's living room. Warmth...security...love. He was offering all of that and more, but it came with a price. Could she afford to love him? Did she have any choice?

She paused in the shadow of the stucco-walled recreation center and stared at the shimmering surface of the swimming pool. It reminded her of the afternoon she and Daniel had splashed and played there, and of all the other wonderful times they'd had together lately. Loving. Being loved. As the images played slowly through her mind, a sense of peace settled over her, and she knew there really wasn't any decision to be made. Being with Daniel, loving him was worth any price— including forgiving Julia Robbins. Daniel was right. She'd been a victim of the past long enough.

An odd rustling in the nearby bushes made her start and glance around uneasily. The area appeared deserted, but she quickly decided it was time to go back inside.

"Too much talk of spies and danger," she muttered, heading for Daniel's backdoor. "You're getting paranoid." But an instant later she sensed a slight movement behind her, and before she could turn or cry out, a hard hand clamped over her nose and mouth. She struggled violently at first, but lack of air quickly took its toll. Consciousness had begun to fade, when a strangely familiar voice growled into her ear.

"Sorry if I startled you, but I was afraid you'd cry out. I'm going to let you go now, but if you try to scream, I'll have to tape your mouth."

She was released and shoved back against the rough surface of the wall. Then Arthur Kingston's arrogant features were crowding her face as he used his lean body to hold her immobile. "Arthur, what are you doing here?" she gasped, trying to push away from his surprising strength.

"I've come to join your party," he said, with a smile that chilled her blood. "Stop struggling, please, or I'll have to hurt you."

Kerith stopped pushing and glared at him, her breathing labored. "What party? What are you talking about?"

"Your little family reunion, of course. Didn't you know your mother and I are old friends?" He laughed, obviously enjoying her confusion. "No, perhaps not. She always was secretive."

"Arthur, you're not making sense." Kerith tried to put some conviction into the words, but it wasn't easy when the whole situation was becoming terrifyingly clear. This man she'd employed for almost a year was somehow connected with Julia Robbins. And the malicious gleam in his eyes didn't speak well of his intent.

"Come along inside, dear, and I'll explain it all." He stepped back, and she saw for the first time he was dressed completely in black, like a man who made his living skulking in shadows. When he took her arm, she instinctively pulled away.

"Still resisting, hmm? I believe I will use the tape. I wouldn't want you to announce our arrival. And perhaps we should have something for those lovely hands." She started to open her mouth to scream, but his hand was quicker, and within moments a wide piece of adhesive tape was sealing her lips.

"Most ungentlemanly of me, I know," Arthur murmured, twisting her arms back, and cinching her hands behind her with something that dug into her wrists. "But necessary. And just in case you decide to get balky, I think you should know I'm armed." He raised his free hand, and the faint moonlight glinted off an evil-looking handgun, its silhouette elongated by what she guessed to be a silencer.

Fear began to pulse heavily in Kerith's veins as she viewed the weapon. Dear Lord, this wasn't a joke. It was appallingly real—as real as the danger Julia had spoken of.

She looked at Arthur, unable to hide the terror in her eyes, and he laughed again. "I see you're beginning to understand. Good. I'd have no compunction about using the gun." He gave her a nudge toward the back-door of Daniel's condominium. "Shall we join the others?"

10

"GOOD EVENING, everyone," Arthur said with mocking cordiality. Using Kerith as a shield, he paused dramatically in the doorway of Daniel's living room. The cold muzzle of his gun pressed into the soft underside of her jaw.

Kerith knew she'd never forget the expressions on the three faces that turned to face them from the couch. Surprise came first, then frozen alarm. Daniel paled visibly and started to rise; Karl swore and started to reach inside his unbuttoned suit coat.

"I wouldn't if I were you," Arthur admonished quickly. The hard nose of the gun forced Kerith's chin up, exposing the vulnerable curve of her throat. "That includes you, Avanti," he added as Daniel lunged off the couch. "I don't want to shoot this lovely lady, but you can change my mind with one suspicious move."

"Damn you. If you hurt her in any way, I'll kill you," Daniel snarled, but he remained where he was.

"There'll be no need for that, as long as you all cooperate. You with the shoulder holster, bring out your weapon slowly, drop it on the floor and kick it over to me."

"Who are you? What do you want?" Karl demanded stonily as he complied.

Arthur retrieved the gun and stowed it in the backpack he had slung over one shoulder. "Perhaps the lady on the couch can answer that for you." He smiled coldly and spoke in perfectly accented German. "*Guten abend, Edelweiss.* How pale you look. I had heard you didn't fare too well on our last assignment."

Julia's complexion turned chalky. "Reardon... Frank Reardon. No, it can't be. They told me you were dead."

"Grossly overstated, my dear. Although there have been quite a few changes in my appearance since you last saw me, thanks to the miracle of cosmetic surgery. And the name is Arthur now. It fits the blond hair better, don't you think?"

"Reardon!" Karl's fists clenched at his sides. "How the hell did you escape that mess in Singapore? Julia nearly died because of you."

"Will someone tell me what's going on here?" Daniel interjected forcefully. He pointed at Arthur. "This guy works for Kerith, are you telling me he's also one of your cohorts?"

"Was," Arthur provided, his thin mouth twisting. "After my last endeavor, I seem to be persona non grata with Interpol and a few other organizations. Julia can tell you all about it, but first I want you two gentlemen facing the wall, with your hands out where I can see them. Quickly now."

When Daniel and Karl were positioned to Arthur's satisfaction on either side of the fireplace, he pulled some odd-looking strips of perforated plastic from the backpack and tossed them to Julia. "You used to be quite efficient with riot handcuffs. Put them on your friends over there. And keep talking, while you're at it; I wouldn't want you plotting anything behind my back." He smirked and urged Kerith further into the room. "Why don't you start by telling your dear daughter, how close you and I once were? How I comforted you in your bereavement and the early months of your pregnancy."

"Any closeness between us was purely a figment of your imagination." As she spoke, Julia rose awkwardly and moved toward Daniel and Karl, the handcuffs in one hand.

Behind her adhesive gag, Kerith swallowed a soft sound of surprise. Where was Julia's cane? A quick look at the couch revealed nothing. Had she dropped it?

Julia stopped behind Daniel and went to work applying the cuffs. When she glanced back at Kerith, however, her eyes seemed to send an oblique message. But when she spoke, her voice held only remorse. "Please believe me, Kerith. I wouldn't have come if I'd known it would endanger you in any way. We were so careful with security."

"Your security was useless," Arthur scoffed. "I've known about your precious daughter all along." He shoved Kerith down on one end of the couch and waved the gun expansively. "Your mother and I worked together before you were born. An amusing little operation in Berlin. At least it was amusing until she got mixed up with the Greek. What was his name?" Arthur stroked his jaw with the tip of the gun. "Oh yes, Jon. Never could understand what she saw in him."

"He didn't have much use for you, either," Julia said scornfully. She finished binding Daniel's hands and shuffled over to repeat the process on Karl.

"Watch the sarcasm," Arthur advised, indicating the far end of the couch with a sharp gesture when she'd finished with Karl's hands. "And have a seat."

As she slowly obeyed, Julia's face grew taut with dismay. "How did you find Kerith? No one aside from me and my direct superior knew she survived the birth. There were no records, no ties. And you were already assigned elsewhere by the time she was born."

"You always did underestimate me." Arthur cautiously maneuvered himself around the glass coffee table to check Julia's handiwork on the men. He kept the gun trained on Kerith's heart. "I offered to take care of you, remember?" He waggled the gun at Kerith. "Including Jon's illegitimate offspring. But you thought you were too good for me."

"That wasn't it, at all," Julia protested. "I refused to marry you because I didn't love you."

"So you said, but I saw the scorn in your eyes." Arthur's features contracted in an ugly sneer. "A man never forgets something like that. Never. When I found out you'd lied about the child being stillborn, I began to keep track of her. Over the years, it became evident you intended to do the same, and I realized I'd found your weakness, your Achilles heel." Satisfied that Karl was securely bound, Arthur edged his way toward Daniel. "Did you know she has an almost fetish-like fascination with you, Edelweiss? She has every one of the birthday envelopes you sent her, and all the correspondence from that discreet bank in Zurich...keeps them in a special, locked file in her office."

Kerith's eyes widened in recognition. So he was the one. He probably did the break-in at the house, too.

Arthur's next statement confirmed her guess. "There was quite a collection of mementos in her house, too. I took great delight in smashing them, the night I . . . visited."

Evidently, that last bit of cruelty was too much for Daniel. With a low growl of anger he jerked around.

Daniel, my love, no! Kerith cried silently, struggling to rise. But she was too late.

Arthur, reacting instinctively to the sudden movement, swung the gun up in an arc and brought it down on the side of Daniel's skull with a sickening thud. Daniel pitched sideways into the wall, bumping his head again, and crumpled to the floor.

A sharp, keening cry echoed in Kerith's throat as she started to go to him. But Arthur stopped her with an aggressive movement of the gun. "Sit down," he snarled. "Or I'll use this gun as it was intended."

Unfortunately, Karl chose that moment to make his move, apparently hoping Arthur was too distracted to notice. Karl had barely taken two steps, before the gun gave a muffled report and the force of a bullet drove him back against the wall. He slid to the floor, knocked unconscious by the impact.

Julia echoed Kerith's cry and tried to rise, but Arthur cut her off with another gesture of the gun. "Stay where you are," he warned. "Both of your men are still alive, at this point. If you want them to remain that way, you'd better cooperate."

Blinking back tears, Kerith frantically surveyed Daniel's still form. His tanned, handsome face looked ashen and incredibly vulnerable, and her love for him made her heart feel as if it would break in half. What a fool she'd been to deny her feelings for so long. She was as irrevocably tied to him as she was to the precious, new life he had helped create within her. A second wave of understanding crested over her.

As irrevocably as she must have been tied to me, Kerith thought, her startled gaze going to the woman sitting at the other end of the couch. *Daniel was right, I haven't been honest with myself—or fair to her.* A new despair tugged at her heart as she gazed again at Daniel, lying unconscious on the cold tile floor. Why did it have to take a disaster like this to make her see the light? The way things looked at the moment, she might never have a chance to tell him of her love.

"Why did you wait until now, Arthur?" Julia inquired, breaking the tense silence. "If you wanted revenge, why didn't you do something sooner? We worked together twice more after Germany, yet you never gave any indication of how you felt."

Arthur sauntered around the coffee table and positioned himself between Kerith and her mother, clearly enjoying his role as dominator. "None of those occasions was right. I wanted you to suffer as I did. Your beloved daughter seemed to be the ultimate means to that end. I was almost certain you'd be retiring—with all that implies—after your narrow escape on our last assignment. So I came here to wait, hoping you'd give in to the urge to meet Kerith, at least once, while the resemblance between you still existed." He tipped the gun

up and used its nuzzle to stroke his upper lip thoughtfully. "I must admit, you are strikingly alike. Although
I think Kerith would make a more interesting bed partner, considering your injuries."

"You animal!" Julia exclaimed with sudden venom.
"Leave her out of it. Just tell me what you want, and let's
get on with this." Her mouth tightened with sarcasm.
"I assume you do have some goal in mind."

Arthur resumed pointing the gun at Kerith. "My goal
is quite simple. I want the documents you received from
the Chinese gentleman just before everything fell apart
in Singapore. As you know, nuclear arms information
is quite valuable, at the moment. I could retire rather
comfortably on the proceeds from selling it."

Julia looked stunned. "What makes you think I have
that? You know I'm required to hand anything like that
over to my superior."

"But you didn't, this time. If you had, Interpol would
have immediately taken certain actions, and I happen
to know they didn't."

A subtle change took place in Julia's attitude. Her
elegant features assumed a crafty arrogance. "Suppose
I did have them. Why would I give them to you?"

She was bluffing. Kerith knew it without bothering
to reason why. And that same instinct told her Julia
wasn't planning to remain passive much longer.

Arthur smiled, still confident of his superiority. "Oh,
you'll give them to me, my dear. Because your lovely
daughter is going to be my guest at a very secluded
hideaway until you do. You see, I have a few scores to
settle with her, too. Including the sprained ankle I got
keeping an eye on her and the Latin-lover boy." He

paused to give Kerith an assessing leer and ran his free hand over the tarnished gold of his hair. "Who can tell? If you take long enough, she might even come to enjoy my attentions."

Kerith saw the attack coming almost before it began. Julia yanked her cane from its hiding place behind a couch cushion and swung it at Arthur with amazing speed. Arthur was too quick for her, though. He was already aiming the gun at her when the cane hit his shoulder a glancing blow.

A wild desperation seized Kerith as she saw the gun jerk, then level with deadly accuracy. She lunged off the couch without a thought for the consequences. Only one thing burned in her mind. She couldn't let him hurt her mother.

She barreled blindly into Arthur's side, using all her weight, knocking him sideways onto the coffee table. There was a tremendous crack of breaking glass, and then Kerith heard the muffled report of the gun just as something slammed into her temple, bringing exploding pain and blackness.

THE DARKNESS held her suspended. She struggled against it, straining to see, fighting for a sense of stability in a world that reeled and floated. Gradually the black lightened to fuzzy gray and she began to hear voices—distant, then nearer and more audible. They were calling her name. She tried to answer, but couldn't make her voice work. A woman's voice, vaguely familiar, said, "I'll never forgive myself for this . . ."

Am I dead? she wondered, twisting in panic.

Then someone's hands settled on her arms, warm, wonderfully strong hands that made the world stop spinning at last. She gave a mighty effort, forced her eyes open and encountered Daniel's marvelous face, tense with concern and only inches away.

"What happened?" she whispered in confusion.

Daniel's face broke into a smile. "Thank God you're awake. No, don't try to get up. I want you to lie still until I can get you to an emergency room."

"Emergency room? Why?" Kerith looked around and discovered she was lying on Daniel's bed. How had she gotten there? The last she remembered, she'd been downstairs... "Arthur!" she cried, as the memory came into sharp focus. "I remember now. He was going to shoot my mother. Where is she? Is she all right?"

"She's fine, thanks to you. Right now she's downstairs helping Karl keep an eye on Arthur."

"But what about you?" Kerith anxiously levered herself up toward him. "When he hit you, and you were lying so still, I thought..." With a little cry, she threw her arms around his neck. "Oh, Daniel, I love you so much. And I was afraid I'd never have the chance to tell you."

His strong arms wrapped around her, pulling her closer as he lovingly nuzzled her ear. "I'm all right, love. Just a bad headache and a large case of self-disgust. If I hadn't been so busy falling in love, I might have noticed something wasn't right about that Kingston character. I was supposed to protect you, and you end up having to do the job yourself. When I came to and saw you throw yourself at that monster..." He shuddered, then raised his head to peer at her questioningly. "That last part, did you mean it?"

"The part about loving you?" She smiled tremulously and nodded.

"Kerith, sweetheart . . ." Daniel started to gather her close again, but a soft knock at the door stopped him.

Julia stood in the open doorway, looking nervous and exhausted. "I'm sorry to bother you, Daniel, but you're needed downstairs. The people we called have arrived."

Daniel sighed and got up reluctantly. "It's all right. Kerith and I will have time to talk later."

"What people?" Kerith inquired. "What's going on down there? Was Arthur . . . ?" She paled. "Did I kill him?"

Daniel stroked her hair reassuringly. "No, he's not dead. Not even badly injured. Although the two of you could have been, when you crashed through that glass table." He tapped her temple lightly, and she winced at the resulting pain. "And you're lucky his elbow didn't connect with your head just an inch or so lower. As for the people downstairs, you might say they're a special cleanup crew. When they're finished, Arthur will have quietly disappeared."

Kerith's eyes widened in alarm. "Disappeared? Where?"

"Karl and I will be accompanying him back to our headquarters," Julia put in quietly. "Arthur has a lot of things to answer for, and we're going to see that he's put out of commission permanently."

"But wasn't Karl shot?" Kerith persisted, still confused.

"It wasn't a serious wound," Julia assured her. "Although I did have a bad moment when that gun went off."

"I really should get down there," Daniel said reluctantly. "Julia, would you stay with her until I get back?"

Julia hesitated, her uncertainty painfully clear. "I will, if Kerith doesn't mind."

Kerith's heart went out to her. "Why would I mind? I think it's time I got acquainted with my mother."

Julia smiled then, but there was a mist of tears in her blue eyes, as she came forward to sit at the side of the bed. "We have so little time, and there's so much I've wanted to say to you."

"Do you have to go?" Kerith asked sadly. She reached out, took her mother's hand, and realized it was the first time they'd touched. So little time . . .

"I must. I won't be responsible for putting your life in jeopardy again. Daniel promised me he'd look after you. Are you in love with him?"

Kerith smiled and nodded.

"Good, then I can go with an easy mind about that at least. Now, what would you like me to tell you?"

THE MOUNTAINS to the east of Las Vegas were limned with the first pink encroachment of dawn as Daniel and Kerith stood at the living-room window and watched a nondescript gray sedan drive off. When it was gone, she turned to him with tears shining in her golden eyes.

"Did I tell you about my name? She chose it." Kerith bit her lip to stop its trembling. "My middle name, Marie, was her name before they changed it. And she took Kerith from the Bible. She . . . she said there was a brook named Kerith, where God hid His prophet Elijah during a time of danger." A few, bright tears escaped, and Kerith swallowed with some difficulty. "When I think of all the years I resented her for hiding from me, and all along I was the hidden one."

"Don't punish yourself anymore." Daniel hugged her close, rocking gently. "You made it up to her tonight. I only wish you could have had more time."

Sniffing back her tears, Kerith snuggled against his strong chest. And the pain eased a little.

"She said we might be able to arrange a secret meeting in a few years. And Karl told me there were ways to get messages to her occasionally, even though she wouldn't be able to reply." She looked up at him and attempted a smile. "Did you know she and Karl are going to retire together? It helps to know she won't be alone."

"But what about you?" Daniel asked, tracing the path of a tear with his fingertip. "You still won't have a family. And whether or not you want to admit it, I think you really do need one."

Kerith didn't have to work at smiling this time. He sounded suspiciously like a man promoting a cause. "I've been thinking of that lately. Would you be interested in sharing yours?"

He went completely still. "Do you mean having the same last name, children, the works?"

Kerith glanced down at her middle. "I think the children part is a foregone conclusion, but yes to the rest." Her breath whooshed out a second later as he swept her up into his arms with a happy shout.

As he looked down at her, his smile rivaled the brilliance of the morning sun peeking over distant mountains. "You're going to love being an Avanti," he proclaimed exuberantly. And when he kissed her, she knew he was right.

Epilogue

KARL BARBER paused outside a private room, one of a select few at the exclusive clinic hidden high in the Alps. His hand went self-consciously to the dark brown hair now adorning his head as he checked his appearance in one of the gilt-framed mirrors lining the plushly carpeted hall. The face looking back at him belonged to a stranger. *So many changes.* He shook his head and rapped on the door.

The voice calling for him to enter belonged to the woman he loved, but the face he saw when he went inside wasn't Julia's. She was still lovely, but in an entirely different way. *Thank heaven they can't change the inside*, he thought, bending to give her a kiss. Soon, even their names would be different, although he had the comfort of knowing they would be sharing their new last name.

"Hello, darling." Julia's smile was still a little uncertain, on the new mouth they'd given her. "I was just enjoying the view." She crossed to a window where lacy curtains stirred on a pine-scented breeze. "Kerith told me she used to love the summers here."

Karl followed her to the window, one hand reaching

into his trousers pocket. "I have something for you." He withdrew a small envelope and handed it to her.

She sank down onto the velvet-cushioned window seat and quickly tore it open. "You bought me a card?" she inquired, drawing out the folded paper. "But it isn't my birth . . ." She stopped, seeing for the first time the pink-cheeked baby depicted on the front. Inside was a formally lettered birth announcement. It began: Mr. and Mrs. Daniel Avanti proudly announce the birth of their daughter, Amanda Marie.

Tears welled in Julia's newly shaped eyes as she held the note to her heart and looked up at him. "Marie," she whispered. "Her middle name is Marie. It . . . it was my name once." The tears overflowed, rolling down the altered line of her cheeks.

Karl used his thumb to gently wipe them away. "Congratulations, Grandma," he said, grinning broadly.

Her answering smile reminded him of the bright splendor of the edelweiss blooming outside the window.

THE FIRST TEMPTATION
OF MAGGIE DAVIS...

Reviewers and readers alike describe her books
as "steamy", "sizzling", "hot".... And now
she's writing for Harlequin!

Watch for *Dreamboat*, an irresistible
Temptation in October.

Available where Harlequin books are sold. DB-1

JAYNE ANN KRENTZ WINS HARLEQUIN'S AWARD OF EXCELLENCE

With her October Temptation, *Lady's Choice*, Jayne Ann Krentz marks more than a decade in romance publishing. We thought it was about time she got our *official* seal of approval—the Harlequin Award of Excellence.

Since she began writing for Temptation in 1984, Ms Krentz's novels have been a hallmark of this lively, sexy series—and a benchmark for all writers in the genre. *Lady's Choice*, her eighteenth Temptation, is as stirring as her first, thanks to a tough and sexy hero, and a heroine who is tough when she has to be, tender when she chooses....

The winner of numerous booksellers' awards, Ms Krentz has also consistently ranked as a bestseller with readers, on both romance and mass market lists. *Lady's Choice* will do it for her again!

This lady is *Harlequin's* choice in October.

Available where Harlequin books are sold.   AE-LC-1

Harlequin Intrigue®

High adventure and romance— with three sisters on a search...

Linsey Deane uses clues left by their father to search the Colorado Rockies for a legendary wagonload of Confederate gold, in #120 *Treasure Hunt* by Leona Karr (August 1989).

Kate Deane picks up the trail in a mad chase to the Deep South and glitzy Las Vegas, with menace and romance at her heels, in #122 *Hide and Seek* by Cassie Miles (September 1989).

Abigail Deane matches wits with a murderer and hunts for the people behind the threat to the Deane family fortune, in #124 *Charades* by Jasmine Crasswell (October 1989).

Don't miss Harlequin Intrigue's three-book series The Deane Trilogy. Available where Harlequin books are sold.

Have You Ever Wondered If You Could Write A Harlequin Novel?

Here's great news—Harlequin is offering a series of cassette tapes to help you do just that. Written by Harlequin editors, these tapes give practical advice on how to make your characters—and your story—come alive. There's a tape for each contemporary romance series Harlequin publishes.

Mail order only

All sales final

Harlequin Historicals

Step into a world of pulsing adventure, gripping emotion and lush sensuality with these evocative love stories penned by today's best-selling authors in the highest romantic tradition. Pursuing their passionate dreams against a backdrop of the past's most colorful and dramatic moments, our vibrant heroines and dashing heroes will make history come alive for you.

Watch for two new Harlequin Historicals each month, available wherever Harlequin books are sold. History was never so much fun—you won't want to miss a single moment!